SAMUEL

Usdi Yona

Jeff Morgan

ISBN: 198126941X
ISBN 13: 9781981269419
Library of Congress Control Number: 2017918703
CreateSpace Independent Publishing Platform
North Charleston, South Carolina

ACKNOWLEDGMENTS

When I first began to contemplate the story of Samuel, I knew where I wanted the story to begin and where I wanted it to end; very carefully, I began to plan the time line of events that were to occur. I felt that this time line should correlate to actual historical events, and I made every effort to make sure this happened. If there are any inaccuracies in my rendition of these events, I assure you it was not intentional.

Even though this book is a work of fiction, I took great care in making it as authentic and accurate as possible. Many of the places described exist or existed during the time frame of the book. Many of the fictional characters in the book are blends of personalities of people I have met throughout my life, but any similarities to actual individuals are coincidental and should not be considered fact.

In the story, the fictional characters interact with actual historical personalities, and I think this gives one the impression that maybe it is meant to be a factual account of the events that occurred. In no way did I attempt to write a true and factual account of actual events.

My primary objective in writing the story of Samuel was simply to create a few characters to whom the reader might relate in a very personal and thoughtful way. There are many complex issues that the story brings to one's attention; how these fictional characters respond to them, I hope, will make the reader ponder these issues as well.

There were many people who helped me throughout the process of writing *Samuel*, and it would be remiss of me not to mention their contributions.

I would first like to thank my wife, Rhonda, for her support and encouragement throughout the process. I am sure she got tired of me reading excerpts to her and asking for her opinion. It was almost a year after I started writing the story before she finally got to read the entire manuscript. She began reading the final manuscript, and I patiently waited three days for her to finish. She handed me the manuscript, and with tears in her eyes, she said, "That's the sweetest story I have ever read!" I knew at that moment that this beautiful story of an old man and a young journalist could touch one's heart. I thank my wife for giving me that moment of feeling a great sense of satisfaction.

Much of the story takes place around the Nantahala National Forest and, in particular, a place called Glen Choga Lodge. This is an actual place that I visited often. The owner of this historical landmark was Don Ezell, and I was fortunate to have him as a dear friend for several years before his passing about a year ago. He was an avid reader and always claimed to be my biggest fan. He was very excited about this new work, *Samuel*, and seemed pleased to have me use his beautiful lodge as the place where Samuel and Jonathan first meet. I thank Don not only for his friendship but also for his inspiration.

To be authentic as possible, I sought help to understand the Cherokee language to correctly translate Cherokee names, places, and phrases. I was very fortunate to have Ashela Lanning to help me in this regard. I thank her immensely for taking the time to help me through this painstaking process.

There were many who contributed by reading excerpts and some who read the entire manuscript. They would give me their honest opinions and suggestions on how I could improve wording or paragraph structure to enhance the book's readability. Lisa Armistead, Sherri McKoy-Interrante, Tobhiyah Emiohe, Doug Brown, Joe Berry, and Rick Harding were a few who gave their time and their opinions unselfishly. I thank them for this, for it was only through their suggestions that this book was brought to a close.

AUTHOR'S NOTE

At times, when fact and fiction are combined, it might be confusing to discern what is real and what is not. I feel sure that many of the notable historical characters mentioned will be recognizable, such as the many presidents whom Samuel meets in the story and possibly some of the civil-rights leaders. However, many names may not be familiar. Paul Dunbar, the writer from Dayton, Ohio; Joseph Rainey, the senator from South Carolina; Lawrence Berender, the lawyer who intervened in Cuba; Federico Laredo Brú, the president of Cuba; E. D. Rivers, the governor of Georgia; Jane Brolin, a judge appointed in New York City; Gifford Pinchot, a conservationist; George Remus, the famous criminal defense attorney from Cincinnati; Will Thomas, the white chief of the Cherokee; and several others are real historical figures who participated in much of the history that this story encompasses. I did take some literary license to incorporate them seamlessly into the plot and time line of the story.

I tell the story that the black poet Paul Dunbar used Wilbur and Orville Wright's printing company to publish many of his first works. This is factual. Of course, Samuel is a fictitious character, but the coincidence of how the fictional story overlaps the factual one is an example of how one may begin to believe the whole story.

I took great care to represent the factual characters truthfully, using much of the same language the historical figures used and their true tenets. If I misinterpreted or misrepresented them factually, it was not done intentionally.

There are many of these overlaps of fact and fiction throughout the story, and I suggest, if one is so inclined, that one research the name of the character or the incident in history mentioned. Not only will it satisfy your curiosity, but it might also enlighten you in a more comprehensive way to the actual era of this story.

The social issues, the mind-set of the populace, and the events that happened during this time motivated me to write *Samuel* in the first place. It was my attempt to understand what went wrong—and what went right—during this tumultuous time in history. I'm not sure I found the answer, but it made me think more about it. I hope that *Samuel* will make you ponder these issues as well, for unfortunately, many of the issues that plagued humanity then still plague us today.

I did not write this book to make a political statement and hope no one interprets it as such, for it was written merely to entertain and make one stop and consider some of the complexities of life that interweave their ways into all humanity.

As Samuel says, "Listen to the stars; listen to their song; listen with your heart."

CHAPTER ONE

Your success lies in your own hands. You must therefore not wait for the grass to become greener by magic. You have the hands to irrigate your own territory by doing what is expected of you!

—Israelmore Ayivor

It was April 24, 1939, when I first set off to meet Samuel. I would be lying if I told you I was excited about going to meet him. With my journalistic skills, I should be interviewing President Roosevelt about the war in Europe—or at least be interviewing Grover Whalen about the opening of the World's Fair here in New York. After all, I am a Harvard graduate.

I'm a journalist for the infamous *New York Times*; I have been for the last two years. My boss, Harold Sims, the executive editor, has had me writing frivolous articles ever since I started. I feel I have earned the right to cover a *real* story, a story with merit, but Sims keeps giving me these discreditable stories to cover—stories that will never be noticed, no matter how well I write them.

I'm mad about having to travel to Aquone, North Carolina, to interview a hundred-year-old negro about his life and then trying to write an article for the *New York Times* that will be interesting and entertaining for the readers. Don't get me wrong; I feel privileged to write for the best newspaper of all time, but I also know a good story from a bad story. I know a story of interest and one that should be ignored. Sims does not.

Therefore, I am on a train heading to Asheville, North Carolina, where I will take a car and drive to Aquone. I have brought only an overnight case and of course my typewriter. Hopefully I can get a few statements from this negro named Samuel and get back to New York by April 30 to attend the official opening of the World's Fair. That's the story I should be covering.

As the train pulls away from the station in New York, I begin to peruse the day's copy of the *Times.* I read it every day from front to back. I know most of the writers and the photographers who work for the paper. I read their articles, study their photos, and critique them in detail. With each one I read, I feel I could have done better. Sims does not give me the chance.

The train rattles down the track and sways gently from side to side. I gaze out the window as the train huffs and puffs, quickly entering a new world of grass and rolling hills. Pastures of cattle and a few fields of corn pass by; small, no-name towns straddle the tracks in places, but the train seems to pass unnoticed.

I read my paper.

The afternoon clamors on, and the train stops occasionally either in this town or the next. I watch as young soldiers in their drab, olive-green uniforms struggle to load their heavy duffel bags onto the train. They smile and joke with one another. I wonder where they are going and what their fates may be. I watch their young faces; most are much younger than I. I see no fear or trepidation in their faces. Their inevitable involvement in the war in Europe does not seem to cross their minds. It is my belief that we will be invested in the war in Europe to thwart Hitler's aggressive actions within a year, and these young soldiers, apparently oblivious to what lies ahead, may soon lose their smiles and their jocularity—and possibly their friends beside them—in the war that is to come.

If the United States becomes involved in this war, then I too will be one of those soldiers. I welcome the opportunity to throw myself into combat and write in detail the story of the heroics of our soldiers. That is a story that warrants my effort.

I watch out the window as the sun lies on the western horizon turning the skies into a painting of turquoise, red, pink, and orange. The clatter of the train and its gentle sway settles into a regular rhythm of monotony that wills me to sleep.

I sleep.

I'm awakened by a knock on my sleeper's door. The porter speaks softly. "Excuse me, sir. Dinner is being served in the dining car." He smiles broadly as I struggle to stand and try to maintain my balance. The train jostles from side to side.

The porter is a negro. He is wearing the customary white tunic and black pants, and he is as dark a negro as I have ever seen. When he smiles, his white teeth gleam, illuminated by the contrasting blackness of his skin. He reaches a strong arm forward to help me regain my balance.

I find myself falling, and I'm grappling for anything near to arrest my fall. Then the porter's hand grabs my arm, stopping the inevitable. His grasp is strong, and he rights me immediately. I glance at the porter as I regain my balance; his smile is gone, replaced with a blank stare of servitude. I say, "Thank you. You are so kind."

He simply nods and moves down the hallway to the next sleeper.

I walk a few cars behind and find the dining car, which is bustling with travelers. Some have already begun their meals, sitting at tables draped in white linen, drinking their wine and champagne.

The men are puffing their cigarettes; a few have cigars, and they fill the car with malodorous fumes, but the diners do not seem to notice. A few soldiers—officers, I presume—sit at one table sipping their beers. Their faces and their conversation appear to be concerned. One of the officers nods a greeting as I pass. I nod in return and sense his worry, his distress about the inevitability of his involvement in the war.

I wonder why these soldiers, these officers, appear to have entirely different demeanors than the young soldiers I witnessed earlier. Could it be their ages? They are considerably older. Or is it that they have experienced the horrors of war, and they fear what they know is to come?

I find an empty table at the far end of the dining car and sit next to the window. I don't know why because as I look out the window, I see nothing but darkness. Occasionally the lights from the dining car are sufficient to illuminate a tree, a telephone pole, or a girder of a bridge as it speeds past, but nothing else.

There is a timid tap on my shoulder, and as I turn, a female voice says, "Excuse me, sir, do you mind if I join you?"

She is a beautiful lady. She is well dressed and about the same age as me. Standing, I suddenly find myself at a loss for words. "Yes, of course. Please, have a seat."

She smiles demurely and sits opposite me in the booth. She offers her hand and introduces herself. "I'm Allison."

I take her hand, introducing myself. "Nice to meet you. I'm Jonathan, Jonathan Newcastle."

Allison says, "I'm sorry to intrude. If you are waiting on others, I can order and have my food delivered to my sleeper. Unfortunately, it seems all the tables are taken." She glances around the dining car to confirm this.

"No, Allison. Like always, I'm traveling alone. Your company is welcome."

"Thank you. And where are you traveling?" she questions as she digs around her purse.

"I work for the *Times*, the *New York Times*, and I'm on assignment to a place called Aquone, in North Carolina."

"How interesting. And what is the story about?"

I wonder if I should tell her the truth or stretch it. Should I tell her I am going to interview a hundred-year-old negro about his life as a slave or that I am to interview a notable dignitary of historic significance? "I'm going to interview Samuel. Samuel Timmons." I leave it at that and hope there are no further questions.

"Samuel Timmons?" Allison says, and for a moment, she is deep in thought and searching her memory. After a few moments, it comes to her. "Oh, *the* Samuel Timmons. Usdi Yona, he is called." And she sits back, quite proud that she remembers.

I nod to confirm, but I think, "Usdi Yona?" I am not aware of that name. What does that have to do with Samuel? I decide I had better read over my notes once again about this assignment. "Do you know Samuel?"

"Oh, no. I've never met him." Allison pats herself as if embarrassed. "I've heard about him though. I think he was a slave at one time and maybe a Cherokee? He seems to have created quite a stir within the political ranks of government."

"And how so?" I question.

"I really don't know. I hear people talking. I live in Atlanta, and my grandfather travels within the political circles. I don't pay much attention to their discussions, but the story of Samuel Timmons I remember."

A waiter approaches and says, "Excuse me, sir, madam. May I interest you in a cocktail?"

I answer quickly. "Yes. I'll have a Barolo wine, and the lady will have?"

"The same," she says, and she smiles.

We drink our wine and have our dinner. We talk amicably over our meal about New York and the inevitable war in Europe, and as the plates are removed and the dining car begins to empty, I say, "It was a pleasure to meet you, Allison. Maybe I will see you again. And you are Allison—"

She smiles and says, "Allison McKinney."

I walk back to my sleeper feeling exhausted. Once there, I fight the urge to sleep. Maybe it's the two glasses of wine I had with dinner, or simply the monotony of travel, but my eyes are heavy. I begin to read my notes.

I study the notes given to me about Samuel Timmons. The notes tell me very little about Samuel or his life. I assume that is why I have been sent on this assignment: to find out more. It still baffles me as to why he is of such interest. Is it simply because he is a centenarian, or is there more to his story?

I fall asleep slowly, though my eyes are heavy, for I am thinking of Samuel, Usdi Yona, and the story he may tell. I lay my notes on the bedside table and close my eyes. With some perturbation, I realize that in the morning, I will meet Samuel and hear his story.

CHAPTER TWO

If you expect nothing, you can never be disappointed.

—Tonya Hurley

Early the next morning, I arrive in Asheville. The sun is shining brightly, but the air is crisp and cool—much cooler than what it had been in New York just the day before. The station is no different than most stations in small towns. The waiting area for the whites is to the right, and the waiting area for the negroes is to the left. I take my overnight case and typewriter, and as promised, a gentleman is waiting expectantly for my arrival. Since there are only a few passengers who disembark and I am the only one with a typewriter in tow, he introduces himself to me. "Hello. Mr. Newcastle, I presume?"

"Yes, I'm Jonathan Newcastle. I assume you are to take me to Aquone?"

The gentleman shakes my hand and responds, "Yes. I'm Thomas Caldwell. My car is around the corner. I'm your driver as well as your photographer. Here, let me take your typewriter for you."

Thomas is short, stocky, and around fifty years old. He is red faced and sweating profusely as he grabs my typewriter and motions me to follow him to his car.

There is little traffic around the depot, and within a few minutes, we are on the road heading south. I ask Thomas if he is familiar with Samuel Timmons and Aquone.

"I've been to Aquone. Been there several times. Never met Samuel, but I know of him. He is kind of a legend in these parts. I live here in Asheville and do freelance work for the local paper, weddings and anything else I can make a buck at. I was surprised when I got the call from the *Times* wanting me to do this. And you? How did you end up here?"

I am looking out the window admiring the emerald-green mountains sprawling on either side. The morning sun is casting its golden glow across the green forests of hemlock, spruce, and fir. We pass a few homesteads, each several miles from the other. The homes are small, log-cabin structures with stacked river-stone foundations. The roofs are moss-covered wood shingles. Small plots of land beside the cabins have been hacked free of the dense vegetation and terraced for the planting of crops. I see smoke escaping from the cabin's rock chimneys but see not a soul.

"Harold Sims, the executive editor at the *Times*, sent me here to do this story about Samuel Timmons. I hope that I can take this afternoon and part of tomorrow and do a quick interview, allow you to take a few photos, and be back on the train heading back to New York by tomorrow night."

Thomas shrugs and says, "Whatever you decide is fine with me."

We drive through an endless maze of mountains and valleys, the scenery becoming redundant. It is two or more hours before we arrive at our destination—a large, two-story log structure named Glen Choga Lodge.

We drive slowly along the long gravel drive toward the log structure. Thomas says, "Well, here we are! Not quite the Waldorf Astoria, but it's the best you'll find around here."

The large log structure is placed well back on the property. A large manicured lawn slopes gently from the front of the lodge downward to a small mountain creek, which feeds a large pond. Several large hemlocks tower above the mountain stream and pond.

Plumes of dust billow around as our car comes to a grinding halt. Thomas retrieves our few bags from the trunk. I stand and stretch, attempting to relieve the kinks in my back from the long drive, and I take in the view. Mountains surround us on all sides. Dense foliage of hemlock, rhododendron, and mountain laurel choke the very breath of the sun. The air is cool, crisp, and fresh. The distinct smell of spruce hangs in the air, and it compels me to reminisce about Christmases past.

A few guests wander aimlessly around the lawn; a few others sit on the large front porch in rockers, appearing to be in a world of their own.

I don't see anyone who could be Samuel.

The proprietor greets us as we enter the lodge. He and Thomas shake hands and share pleasantries, having met on several occasions in the past. Thomas introduces me to the proprietor, and as we shake hands, the proprietor says, "Nice to meet you, Mr. Newcastle. It is a pleasure to have you stay with us. I'm Alexander Steuart. My wife, Margaret, and I hope you find your accommodations satisfactory." He then helps Thomas and me with our few bags and shows us to our rooms.

As the proprietor turns to leave, I question him. "Mr. Steuart, I am here to interview a man named Samuel Timmons. Has he arrived, by chance?"

The proprietor smiles and nods. "Yes. Samuel arrived last night. I think he is currently taking a walk. He enjoys taking walks in the woods. He should be back in time for dinner. If I see him, I will tell him you have arrived."

"Thank you. That's very kind," I say.

It's late in the afternoon. Thomas and I eat dinner in the dining room. There are several guests eating as well. We sip our wine and engage in idle conversation with the others. Samuel has yet to arrive.

I stroll onto the porch to enjoy the fresh air and to distance myself from the chatter. The air is crisp and cool. There is no breeze. The cicadas are singing their symphony as the lightning bugs dance in the still air. The stars fill the sky above in their brilliant splendor.

It's so unpretentious yet so beautiful.

"Do you hear the stars as well?" A voice from the shadows questions me.

Startled, I turn and stare into the dark shadows to find the source of the question.

"Sorry. I don't understand. Hear the stars? I see them, but I do not hear them. But you hear them as well?" I say and step into the shadows beside the shadowy figure. I think it must be Samuel.

He is a small man. His hair is long, unkempt, and white as snow. He has a long white beard that is matted and tangled. His skin is dark, as black as charred wood, and weathered. He smiles a gentle smile and says, "Yes. Their song is even more beautiful than their brilliance. Close your eyes and listen—not with your ears, but with your heart." Samuel says this with such conviction that I immediately close my eyes and try to listen as he says. I only hear the steady rhythm of my beating heart.

Embarrassed, I say, "I seem to be deaf to their song. You must be Samuel. Samuel Timmons."

"Yes. I am Samuel." He stands and reaches out his hand in greeting.

"I'm Jonathan. Jonathan Newcastle. I write for the *New York Times*, and I have come to Aquone to meet you, Mr. Timmons."

"Please, Mr. Newcastle. Call me Samuel."

"Of course, and please call me Jonathan."

Samuel sits back down in his rocker and pulls a corncob pipe from the breast pocket of his jacket. He fills the bowl carefully with a stringy tobacco. He lights it with a strike of a match and takes a deep draw of the pipe. The bowl glows red.

"So Jonathan. Why do you come all this way to meet me? What is so interesting about me that warrants your attention?"

"I would like to hear your story, Samuel. Someone who has lived as long as you must have an interesting story to tell."

Samuel smiles and takes another deep draw on his pipe. He nods and says, "If your heart is deaf to the melody of the stars, maybe it will be deaf to me as well."

I am immediately intrigued by his apparent wisdom and honesty. I say, "Maybe eventually I too will hear the stars sing."

Samuel cocks his head inquisitively my way. He seems to be judging my sincerity. He asks meekly, "Where do you want me to begin?"

"I should think the beginning would be a good place to start, would it not?" And I laugh.

Samuel does not laugh; instead, he shakes his head and says, "I am an old man, Jonathan. I have lived a little over a hundred years. If I start at the beginning as you suggest, it will be quite a lengthy tale."

"I'm sure it will, Samuel, but I am prepared to hear it in total."

Samuel studies me once again and then nods his head, saying yes. He says, "Jonathan, it is a story that may offend some and may anger others, and some of the things I have done, I may not be ready to reveal."

"Samuel, you are free to tell me what you like. Whatever you tell me, if you request that it not be printed, then it will not. That I promise."

"Very well, Jonathan. I will start at the beginning."

CHAPTER THREE

The quieter you become, the more you can hear.

—Ram Dass

The sun has only barely risen when I return to the porch to meet Samuel the next morning. There is a layer of fog that hugs the lawn. The tall hemlocks appear as spires suspended above the opaque layer of cloud. I hear the ducks splashing and hear their quacks, but the fog hides them from view. Samuel sits in a rocker, smoking his pipe, waiting to begin his story.

"Good morning, Samuel," I say and then study his features in more detail with the daylight that was not afforded the night before. His blackened skin is weathered with deep creases and furrows covering his brow. He smiles.

"Good morning, Jonathan. Will you walk with me?"

"Yes. Of course, Samuel. Where do you want to walk?"

Samuel gives that all-knowing smile and says, "We will walk till we find what we are searching for."

I am already beginning to tire of his constant riddles and questions, but I indulge him. "And what are we searching for?"

"The truth."

He stands and waves me by his side, and we start walking down the front lawn toward the pond that still is hidden by the fog.

I question Samuel as we walk. "Samuel, forgive me for being so blunt, but I am curious. You are a negro, yet your hair is not as a negro's, and you speak different as well; but you are a negro, are you not?"

Samuel glances at the back of his hand as if trying to determine the color himself but does not answer.

We stand at the edge of the pond, and he points to the mirrored surface of the water, where both our mirrored images stare back. He questions me. "What do you see, Jonathan?"

I assume he is referring to our reflections on the surface. I say, "I see you and me."

"And do you see a negro?"

"Yes. I see a negro and myself."

"Please, Jonathan. You must look deeper. Consider the pond itself. What do you see?"

I stand staring into the pond but not knowing what I should be looking for. I shake my head and say, "I'm not sure what you want me to see."

"Look deeper, Jonathan. Do you not see the fish that swim side by side? The red-colored rock that lies on the bottom, the crawfish that is trying to hide from the fish, the gentle sway of the grass that sprouts from the sandy bottom?"

"Yes. I now see the fish," I say. I strain even harder trying to see the rest of what Samuel has described.

"See, Jonathan, you must look deep. To answer your question as to whether I am a negro, I will tell you to look deep in here." And he pounds his chest. "Look deep into my soul. You will find your answer there."

I think about what he has said and stare at the old man standing before me. Almost apologetically I say, "I see a kind man."

Samuel smiles and begins telling me his story.

"I was born a slave in March of 1838. My father was Ezekiel Timmons, and my mother was Sarah. Both were slaves, and their parents were as well. From my earliest memory, I worked the cotton fields by my mother's side, as did my father. The only thing we owned were our names and the love we had for one another.

"It was a hard life, a life filled with fear, misery, and hopelessness. We were the property of Ethan Jackson, and we worked his fields of cotton from dawn to dusk. If one became ill or was unable to work, there would be a lashing. We normally would have Sundays off, and that is when I would l go to the river to fish, to supplement our rationings of food. Corn chowder and bean soup were the norm.

"The lashings that were administered to us were common. Most were so severe as to put the unfortunate recipient of the punishment near death. I was beaten severely several times, even before I turned fourteen years of age.

"Tattered rags were our clothes. These rags were given to us by our master. There were no shoes. When I outgrew a tattered pair of pants, they were removed from me and handed down to another slave a bit smaller than myself. If I was lucky, there was someone a little older, a little larger, who had outgrown his pants as well, and I would receive his.

"Adult slaves wore their clothes till they were falling off their bodies, and only then were they given materials to mend the clothes they had. If they were lucky, they were given hand-me-downs from the master's family.

"The field master—we called him Captain—was ruthless. He lived for the moment to give one of us a lashing. He seemed to enjoy inflicting as much pain as possible. We tried to distance ourselves from him for fear of becoming the recipients of his anger."

Samuel turns and begins walking toward the woods, and I follow beside him. He is walking slowly; stopping occasionally, he studies the bark of a tree or a small insignificant stone that he takes notice of. He seems to be thinking about the fear and terror of the Captain.

"He raped my mother. He raped her many times over the years. I could only watch from the corners of our one-room shanty as the Captain had his way with her. She would weep silently. I wanted to help her, stand before Captain, and strangle the life from him, but my mother knew if I tried, then I too would be hung, as my father had years before. I could only watch and weep the same helpless tears as her.

"During my early years as a child, my mother would talk about her dreams of one day being free. Free from the pain and misery of being a slave. Even then at that early age, I seemed to be aware that her dream for freedom was not for her but for me. With her musings of freedom, I began to have hope for freedom as well.

"Captain continued to inflict pain on us all. His raping continued, and my hate grew. I was thirteen, and one night, my mother wept hysterically. I begged her to tell me what was wrong, what terrible thing had Captain done to her, but what she told me was worse than I could have imagined.

"She explained that even though it tormented her that I may have to live as a slave for the rest of my life, what she feared most was that I would become filled with so much hate, so much anger, that I would lose the ability to have compassion. That night she began to organize a plan for my escape to freedom."

Samuel and I walk a small trail, climbing higher into the wooded mountains. The sun bends through the tight canopy of oak and poplar above us. The fog that had hugged the ground earlier is now just a memory. Birds are chirping, flitting from one tree to the next. A squirrel chatters loudly as we pass beneath the branch on which he is sitting.

I glance at Samuel, and he has a twinkle in his eye and a slight smile on his lips. I ask him, "With all the pain that was inflicted on you, your father, and mother, do you not still hate, want revenge?"

"If I allowed the hate, the anger, to consume me, then I would have never been free. It would have owned my soul, much the same as my slave master had owned me. That's what my mother had feared the most. I will never submit to being enslaved by anyone again nor by the shackles of hate and anger. I choose to use my freedom and forgive."

I nod and say, "So you were able to escape, secure your freedom?"

Samuel nods, saying, "Yes, but it was not easy." He continues his story.

"The plantation we worked was only a mile from the Savannah River, just outside of Edgefield, South Carolina. That was where I would fish. I became quite good at that. My mother began saving what little provisions she could, and I would bring home fish, which we smoked to preserve. In October of 1852, I packed what I could fit in a small bag slung over my shoulder and kissed my mother good-bye. I left in the dark of night and headed north, following the Savannah River. I was going to seek refuge with the Cherokee.

"Rumor was that the Cherokee would adopt runaway slaves into their tribe, but then we had also heard that the Cherokee had grown wise and at times would simply sell the runaways back to white slave owners for money. I had no other choice but to head north, keeping the river to my left. Once in the Appalachians, I might find the Cherokee who might give me refuge.

"I was only fourteen years of age, and even though I had lived a lifetime of pain and suffering, my experience outside the plantation was minimal.

"I almost gave up. I almost died within the first week of my running away.

"I had no information as to how far I would need to walk or how long it may take me. My mother had simply told me to keep walking north until I saw the mountains, mountains so tall that they would appear to touch the clouds. She explained that is where I might find my freedom. It was probably fortunate that I was unaware of the almost unsurmountable distance I would need to walk and naive as to the hardship and misery I would have to endure, for if I had known what lay ahead, I may have never left the horror of slavery. I had no map to guide me. I only had the Savannah River, which I kept on my left while walking upstream.

"The Savannah River during that time was used to transport goods from inland cities to the ports located in Savannah. There were constant barges loaded with bales of cotton, tobacco, and other goods floating south. White men piloted these barges downriver. The danger of any of them discovering me was great. The barges would stop regularly at small docks along the banks of the river. These docks were busy with white men loading more goods onto the barges, and I had to use much care in avoiding these areas.

"I was in constant fear that I would be captured and returned to my owner. I had no papers to say I was a free man. If captured, I would have been returned to my rightful owner and then most likely beaten till near dead. That was the way it was. This I knew without doubt.

"Most of the time, the terrain I traveled was thick with vegetation. It made walking most difficult. I did not want to stray far from the river for fear of losing my direction. I found that a hard day's journey might only accomplish four or five miles. I became increasingly discouraged and fearful I might fail in my endeavor. Every day as the sun filled the sky, I would look north and pray I would see the mountains that touched the clouds.

"Snakes were abundant, and on several occasions, I came dangerously close to one of these ending my journey for sure. I had no torch to light my way, so in early evening, I would have to find a suitable place to bed for the night. Usually this amounted to nothing more than a damp piece of ground with a tall tree's trunk to lean against as I slept sitting up.

"Within a week, the provisions that my mother and I had hoarded for a year were gone. I began to fish the river to survive. It seemed most of my effort was spent to merely survive, and only a small portion of my effort moved me farther north and toward my freedom.

"The river became narrower, and barge traffic became less, and I felt I must be approaching the headwaters of the Savannah. I became heartened by this small observation.

"I followed the river till it began to branch in many directions—small streams that went this way and that—and I would choose the one that seemed the most obvious choice, but I had no way of knowing where it might lead. I would tell myself, how can you be lost if you are free? Was I not looking for freedom?

"In November of 1852, I was in the Appalachians. The mountains were rugged and tall; they appeared to touch the clouds, just as my mother had said. I would walk for days and see no one. I stayed close to streams and fished them regularly. I would find crawfish and frogs. I managed to satisfy my hunger, and this brought me great satisfaction, but the nights began to be bitter cold, and I began to fear what was to come and what I might have to endure.

"I was in Tsatu-gi, the Chattooga River. I find it odd now because at the time I did not know, but Tsatu-gi, Chattooga, in Cherokee means 'has crossed the river.' I crossed that river, and then the streams and rivers stayed on my right. The moment I crossed the Chattooga, I felt I entered a new land, a land where I would be free.

"The terrain itself was as rugged and choked with rhododendron and mountain laurel as I had ever seen. The nights grew colder, rain turned to sleet, and the streams seemed void of fish. I became hungry and very cold. I began to wonder if I would survive.

"I wondered how long and how far I had been walking. The days grew shorter; the nights grew longer and much colder.

"I wandered through the mountains, following the streams as best I could, and found myself heading north and west into an area that was known to be the land of the Cherokee. It was a land of steep and rugged mountains, fertile valleys, and mountain streams."

Samuel looks at me and questions, "Do you know what 'Cherokee' means?"

"No, Samuel, I do not believe I do."

"I was told by my Cherokee father that it means 'those who live in caves.' That must have been the time I became Cherokee because I spent many nights in caves." Samuel laughs.

I look at Samuel and ask a question I feel is most personal. "Samuel, did you not still think of and worry about your mother?"

Samuel stops and stares at me as if questioning what I had just said. With the back of his weathered hand, he wipes a tear from his eye and says, "I cried every night, not for me but for her, for I was living her dream."

Samuel and I have been walking for half a day, and we rest our weary legs by a stream. The water bounces down the rocky streambed, splashing and tumbling in cascades of white. We both sit, silent, savoring our own thoughts and emotions.

It may have been the strenuous walk, the warmth of the noon-day sun, or the monotonous sound of the stream, but unwillingly, I fall asleep. It's a deep sleep—a sleep that produces dreams of mountains, fish, and a boy named Samuel.

When I wake, I'm unsure where I am, and I fumble about to regain some sense. Samuel is lying on a flat rock in the stream. He is lying on his back, his head facing the skies above him. He appears to be counting something in the air. I question him. "Samuel, what are you doing?"

He does not stop counting and does not look my way; he says, "I'm counting stars."

"Samuel, there are no stars to count. Not during the day. There are no stars to be seen!"

Samuel responds quietly, "I've tried to count the stars at night, Jonathan. It is too formidable a task to achieve. I find it much easier to count them during the day." And he continues counting the unseen twinkles.

It's at that moment that I begin to question my own ability to capture his story, the sense of Samuel. I find the story strange, exotic, and mystic, but I'm finding it hard to capture the words that express the depth, the spirit, of Samuel. I begin to count the unseen stars as well.

Samuel stands and gingerly walks through the cold mountain stream to where I sit. He gives me that gentle, caring smile and says, "Let's walk. I've got more to tell."

I question him as I stand. "Samuel, what do you call this mountain? The one we have been walking on all day?"

Samuel smiles and says, "It's Alexander Steuart's mountain." And he chuckles a big belly laugh. Then he explains further. "We are actually just east of the famous Wa-Ya. We call it Wayah. It means 'wolf' in Cherokee. We are just east of Wolf Mountain."

I reproduce the sound of the name, and it sounds pleasant to my ears. *Wayah.* I then say aloud, "And are there wolves?"

Samuel grins and says, "They are no longer there, but they were once. They were red wolves. They were beautiful animals. Everyone considered themselves lucky if they ever got to witness one. I was fortunate and got to see many. I wish you could have seen them, Jonathan. They would have been worth your attention more than this poor old man you seem to ponder."

"Yes, Samuel, I wish I could have seen them. Maybe we can walk Wayah one day. I would like to see where these red wolves lived."

Samuel stops and studies a small, red mushroom on the forest floor but answers my question. "I will take you there, Jonathan, but not today. This mushroom is quite tasty. Would you like to try?" Samuel stoops and breaks the mushroom's stem at the ground.

Samuel smells the red dome of the mushroom and takes a bite. He smiles broadly as he chews and hands me the remaining portion.

I too sniff the portion in my hand, as Samuel had, and then nibble a small bite. It tastes like cherries jubilee. I say, "It is very good. What is it called?"

Samuel says, "Di Wa Li." And he smiles as we once again begin to walk, searching for the truth.

CHAPTER FOUR

Be kind, for everyone you meet is fighting a harder battle.

—Plato

Samuel and I walk all day. I hear more stories of his life searching for the Cherokee and his freedom. They are strange stories—stories filled with adventure and hardship—yet Samuel tells it as though his life is as common as the next.

The sun is setting, and the forest darkens quickly. I begin to worry. I say, "Samuel, are we heading back? It's getting dark, and we have not eaten all day."

He slows his steps and turns his head. The light of day has diminished so that all I can see is a profile of tangled hair and a bent frame of an old man. He says, "Jonathan, I hope you will hear the stars tonight."

We arrive back at Glen Choga as the full moon peeps over the eastern horizon. The soft illumination sends strange moon shadows across the lawn of the lodge. We stroll onto the porch. I ask,

"Samuel, will you please have dinner with me? I would very much like to hear more of your story."

Samuel shakes his head as if saying no. He says, "They see a negro, Jonathan. They do not look deep, deep in here as you." And he taps his chest. "I am not allowed to eat at your table. I must eat on the back porch, beside the kitchen. That is the way it is."

I was at a loss for words. I did not realize, did not think about, the fact that he was a negro. They were not allowed to eat with the whites. That was the way it was. That was why he never showed at dinner the night before.

"Then, Samuel, can I eat on the back porch with you? I want to hear the rest of the story."

Samuel smiles and says, "It's really quite nice on the back porch. I know the cook."

Samuel and I walk to the back porch, and he exchanges greetings with the kitchen staff. They are negro as well. I notice that they treat Samuel with the respect that is usually afforded only to dignitaries. He introduces me as "Jonathan, a famous journalist for the *New York Times*."

The kitchen staff brings a bottle of wine and pours a sip for Samuel to approve. They drape a white linen tablecloth over a wooden crate and place two candles upon it and begin to set the makeshift table with their finest dinnerware.

I stare into the kind eyes of Samuel as he sits across from me. There is a twinkle in his eye as if he is savoring the moment, yet I see a glimpse of torment and sorrow as well. I ask him timidly, "What is the sorrow you still carry?"

He smiles and says, "You learn fast, Jonathan. Maybe you *will* hear the stars tonight."

He takes his corncob pipe from his pocket and once again lights the stringy tobacco. He inhales deeply, and as he exhales the acrid smoke, he answers, "I find it to be a too formidable task to count my sorrows. I choose to count the blessings, as I do the stars of the day."

I take a sip of my wine and study the strange old man across from me with growing curiosity. I would normally be thinking of how I would interpret the story given me, how I could make it a story that would capture the attention of my readers, but now I feel captured myself. I am captured by his grace, by his kindness, and by his wisdom. I question him. "Samuel, you seem so wise, wise of the world. Where did you attain this knowledge? From your years as a slave? Or was it the years you lived as a Cherokee?"

Samuel takes another long draw from his pipe and says, "As a slave, I learned how to survive. As a Cherokee, I learned how to live."

I sip my wine, and as hard as I try, I cannot formulate the words that describe the emotions that I feel. I am a journalist, but I cannot begin to describe the humbleness, the wisdom, the power, the magnetism that Samuel possesses. I am at a loss for words.

Samuel begins to tell more of his story.

"The weather had turned foul. There was only light snow, but it was very cold. I wandered into the area known by the Cherokee as Yunwitsule-nunyi. It is not far from here, just south, maybe twenty miles. Yunwitsule-nunyi means 'where the man stood' in Cherokee. The mountains are some of the tallest and the weather most unforgiving. I suffered greatly.

"Occasionally I would hear a musket fire in the distance. Cherokee, I assumed, shooting deer, turkey, and possibly bear. I had seen many of each. At times, I was close enough to these Cherokee hunters to hear their conversations, but they spoke in their native language, and I did not understand.

"I was terribly afraid of being discovered. I had walked all that way to find the Cherokee, and now that I had found them, I was unsure. I wondered what they might do to me if I was found, so I stayed hidden and watched them with interest.

"It was toward the end of November, maybe even early December, and I continued to stay in Yunwitsule-nunyi. I stayed high in the mountains, sleeping in a cave, coming out during the warmer times of day to fish and forage for black walnuts, hazelnuts, persimmons, pawpaw, and artichokes.

"I watched the Cherokee who came into the mountains to hunt. I studied them from a distance, learning their hunting and trapping techniques. They were very ingenious in their design of traps. Once they had placed their traps and left, I would approach and study the makings of the traps in detail, and then I began to make my own. I became quite adept at catching rabbit and squirrel. I knew then that I would never go hungry.

"I had very few tools at my disposal. I still had the knife my mother had given me, and I scavenged where the Cherokee would hunt. I found spent arrows, a hatchet, and a small handsaw lost or inadvertently left by the Cherokee. I fashioned myself a large staff, a six-foot-long hickory pole with a sharpened point. This I carried wherever I went. I found it quite useful to spear fish, toads, and other small game.

"It was early spring, April, when I first saw Peter. He was a young Cherokee boy, two years younger than I. He was walking the woods of Yunwitsule-nunyi, hunting with a bow and a quiver of arrows. I don't think he was hunting. To him it was just a game, a childish sport of stalking small game and shooting an arrow but not trying to hit the target. I followed him, staying hidden. I was hoping to retrieve some of his arrows that he could not find.

"The boy inadvertently walked upon two small bear cubs. The boy was startled, as well as the cubs, and I watched what might happen. The mother bear at that moment came bolting out of a rhododendron thicket with such vengeance and speed that I thought for sure the young boy would be killed.

"Without much thought, I rushed into the clearing, yelling, screaming obscenities, and swinging my hickory staff at the attacking bear. One of my reckless swings caught the sow just at the left ear and sent the huge bear retreating into a thick cover of dog hobble.

"The young Cherokee boy was Peter. His spiritual name was Degataga, which means 'standing together.' He said I saved his life."

Samuel glances at me and sees I am waiting anxiously to hear the rest. He smiles and says to me, "Funny thing, Jonathan. Peter claimed I saved his life that day, but I feel, even to this day, that he actually saved mine."

Our dinner is served, and we both eat till we cannot eat anymore. I am curious as to Samuel's opinion on the war in Europe. I question him as he once again lights his pipe. "Samuel, do you have an opinion on the war in Europe? Do you think the United States will enter the war?"

Samuel thinks for a minute or two as he puffs his pipe. He nods my way and says, "Unfortunately, Jonathan, mankind will always find a reason to battle. I personally cannot fathom what would be so egregious to warrant a war, but then again, I look at life a little different than most."

I say in return, "But Samuel, Hitler is claiming that his people are superior and all the others must die. He is persecuting the Jews; he is killing the Jews. He is marching across Europe, conquering one nation after another. He must be stopped!"

"Yes, Jonathan, I am aware of Hitler's atrocities, and I too have been persecuted just for my race. My father and mother suffered and eventually were killed just because they were negro. Unfortunately, Jonathan, peace cannot be achieved through violence; it can only be attained through understanding."

I look at Samuel, and with anger I say, "Samuel, you fought for your freedom. You had the right to fight for the atrocities that were done to you and your family. And you deny the Jews and the people of independent nations the same right to fight?"

Samuel smiles and very calmly says, "Jonathan, I never fought for my freedom; I simply sought my freedom. I do understand the dilemma we all face with this matter, but the real and lasting victories are those of peace and not of war."

I want to argue. I want to convince Samuel that he is wrong, but something in me begins to realize that maybe he is right. It is a very complex concept, one that I will have to ponder for hours and maybe even days before I can get a real grasp on the idea: peace through understanding of someone like Hitler. Samuel adds, "Jonathan, you did not fight or argue with the establishment, demanding that they allow me to join you for dinner with the *whites*. Instead, you joined *me* on the back porch. It was a beautiful dinner, was it not?"

I think about Samuel's question and realize his subtle point. I smile and say, "Samuel, it was the best dinner I think I have ever had."

I thank Samuel for a wonderful day and walk back through the lodge toward my room. I see Thomas, my photographer, sitting in the dining room, sipping on what appears to be whiskey and smoking a cigar. I say, "Thomas. So sorry. I've been busy with Samuel. I hope you have found something to entertain you."

Thomas smiles and says, "Jonathan, I'm paid whether I sit here and sip my whiskey or chase after you and Samuel. Just let me know where and when you want me to take pictures, and I'll be there."

"Yes, Thomas. I will let you know." I walk to my room thinking about my conversation with Samuel. Once in my room, I sit at my typewriter and type notes. I type thoughts, ideas, revelations, stories, adventures, and questions as well. The typewriter clicks and taps out endless letters, words, sentences, and paragraphs; all seem inadequate to capture the persona, the spirit, of the kind man Samuel. Frustrated and feeling like a failure, I sleep.

CHAPTER FIVE

When I discover who I am, I'll be free.

—Ralph Ellison

I was up before sunrise this morning. I feel refreshed, alive, and anxious for the day's adventure. I am to meet Samuel once again on the front porch at sunrise. My dress shoes, the only ones I brought, were muddy and scratched, and the soles seem half of what they had been when I arrived, but I slip them on anyway. I wish now I had considered bringing some adequate walking shoes.

I put on my tweed sport coat, also the only one I thought to bring. It is my favorite (it's the only one I own), but the air is much cooler this morning. I feel I need the extra layer against the chill. I look at myself in the vanity mirror and almost laugh at the sight. I have not shaved since leaving New York. My hair is unwashed, and even though I brought a comb, I have not thought to use it. The dress shirt that had looked so debonair a few days before is now wrinkled and spotted with filth. I wonder what Samuel will think about seeing such a spectacle.

Samuel is not sitting in his usual rocker on the porch as I arrive to meet him. I am immediately concerned. I glance across the front lawn, and I see the centenarian standing at the edge of the pond. I watch him as he gazes into the mirrored surface, and I can only imagine what he is thinking. I *know* he is looking deep. Probably watching the two fish, the crawfish, and the blades of grass. I stroll slowly in the early morning dawn, the dew of the grass wetting my scratched oxfords, my sport coat pulled tightly around me to thwart the chill. I approach quietly as Samuel stares into the pond.

Before I say a word, Samuel speaks. "There it is, Jonathan, my boy. There it is! I be damned!" And without taking off his boots or rolling up his trousers, he wades into the chilly waters. He is smiling, almost laughing as he wades to the middle of the pond, the water to his waist. He stops and studies the water beneath him, and then in one quick motion, he plunges his head into the icy water. A second later the old man emerges, his hair and beard soaked, hanging limp against his frail frame. He is laughing uproariously and brandishing a tarnished bugle.

He walks hurriedly from the waters and with excitement begins to tell me what he has found. "Jonathan. This is it! I have been searching this pond for almost eighty years to find this bugle." And he stops and inspects it as he stands on the dry ground beside me, water dripping and puddling around the two of us.

I scold him. "Samuel, you're going to kill yourself. You're wet. It is so cold!"

"Jonathan, please, I must tell you the story of this bugle."

Samuel is elated. He keeps staring at the tarnished bugle, and we both walk hurriedly back toward the lodge. Once there, he sits in his rocker and begins to tell me the story.

"My brother Peter, Degataga—he was the young Cherokee that I saved from the bear. In the years following, he and I became like brothers. I taught him how to fish, and he taught me the Cherokee ways as well as their language. We fished this pond as youngsters and well into our adult years. During the Civil War, there was a small group of Union soldiers that had set their camp at this very spot. Peter and I came upon them when we came to fish one morning. We kept our distance and did not make ourselves known to them. We knew there were Confederates in the area, and we could only imagine what might happen if the two groups happened upon one another. Peter and I were here to fish at daybreak, but when we saw the Union soldiers camping, we hid in the woods and watched with interest.

"Just at daybreak, a young Union soldier emerged from a tent with his bugle and began to play reveille. Both Peter and I looked at each other, thinking how stupid this seemed. The blaring sound carried for at least a mile, alerting everyone, even the Confederates, if nearby. As the young soldier belted out his rising melody, an officer emerged from another tent and scolded the young soldier with vengeance. The officer grabbed the bugle from the boy and tossed it into the pond. The officer slapped the young soldier across the face and pounced on him with such a rage, I thought for sure the young soldier would be killed. There was a crack of a rifle, and the officer fell to the ground, and a moment later, another shot rang out, and the young soldier who had been blowing the bugle fell beside the dead officer. A small group of Confederates rushed the camp, and in just a matter of a few minutes, every Union soldier was killed. It was most terrifying to watch.

"After that horrific battle, Peter would never come back to this pond to fish. He said he could hear the bugle playing whenever he came within a mile of the place. The sound of the bugle seemed to put so much fear in Peter that he never seemed to be the same as he once was. I had always thought that if I could retrieve that bugle from the pond, maybe the sound Peter heard in his mind would stop. I've looked for this bugle for close to eighty years."

Samuel smiles, stares at the tarnished instrument, and says, "Peter has been gone for close to eighty years now himself. I hope now he can rest in peace, no longer having to listen to that bugle."

The sun peeps over the eastern ridges, and a blanket of golden warmth falls upon us as we sit on the porch. Birds dart from tree to tree, sending fleeting shadows all around us. Samuel sits in his rocker, puddles of water pooling beneath him. He is still holding the bugle in his lap. He seems to be reminiscing. I assume he is thinking about his good friend, his brother Peter. I say, "It appears you and Peter were very close. You seem to miss him greatly."

Samuel nods and says, "Peter was the only person in my entire life who treated me as an equal. He accepted me for who I was without reservation. He loved me as a brother, and I did him as well. I do miss him. It has been eighty years or so since he passed, but I still think of him often. As years passed after his death, I began to think of him less often, and then I would feel guilty that I would let that happen. Dealing with the death of someone that is such a part of your life is difficult. There is little respite from the pain, even with time."

I nod, and there is an air of sorrow that envelops the porch where we sit. I question him. "May I ask how Peter came to his demise?"

A look of woeful sadness fell upon Samuel's face, a look of so much sorrow that I think Samuel may begin to cry. Samuel says, "I killed him, Jonathan."

I am shocked beyond words. I do not know what to say and am not sure even what to think. I stare at the old man who sits across from me, and I cannot imagine how it can be true. In just the short time I have known Samuel, I have come to realize that he is probably the gentlest and kindest man I have ever known. Yet he now tells me he killed his friend, his brother whom he had loved. I say, "How can this be, Samuel?"

Samuel nods and says, "That is a story I will tell you later, Jonathan. Today I want to take you to where I was raised as a Cherokee. My old home place on Wa-ya, Wolf Mountain."

Samuel stands and says, "Forgive me, Jonathan, but I should change out of these wet clothes before I catch a fever. It will just take a moment. Then we will begin our trek to Wa-ya."

I wait in the bright sunshine and think about what Samuel has just told me about Peter. It just cannot be true.

Samuel returns wearing a plaid wool jacket; a soft, wide-brimmed felt cap; and overalls. He is smiling broadly and puffing on his corncob pipe as he approaches me. He looks at me and says, "Jonathan, your sense of fashion is even inferior to mine." He shakes his head and laughs to himself.

Thomas, my photographer, steps onto the porch as Samuel and I begin to take leave. I introduce Thomas to Samuel, and they exchange pleasantries. Samuel invites Thomas to join us for our walk, but he apologetically declines. Instead, he suggests taking a few photographs of Samuel in the beautiful morning light. Samuel agrees.

The photo session seems to go well, and before long, Samuel and I begin to amble down the long, gravel drive heading in the direction of Wa-ya.

I am quite amazed at the physical abilities of Samuel. He is a little over one hundred years old, but I feel he can outwalk me. I am twenty-five and consider myself in relatively good shape, but Samuel never seems to tire. He walks slowly, his gait a little erratic at times, and his back is bent with age, but I am amazed at his abilities.

I have no idea how far we had walked the day before, but it must have been a considerable distance, for we walked the entire day. I assume we will walk the same today, and I begin to wonder if I will be physically able. I look at my shoes and again wish I had thought to bring something more adequate.

Samuel says, "Let me tell you about my Cherokee home." He continues his story.

"My adoptive Cherokee father was a *didanawisgi*, a Cherokee medicine man of the highland tribe of which I became a part. His name was Gawonii, which means 'He is speaking.' He was the grandfather of my brother Peter and was considered by the Cherokee to be the wisest of them all. When I first met Gawonii, I thought he was the oldest human I had ever met. Now as I look back, he was most likely only about fifty years of age, half of mine today, but he carried with him triple that in experience and knowledge. He was very spiritual and helped all the Cherokee maintain their harmony with their mind, body, and spirit. He helped the Cherokee with their *tohi*, which means 'wellness' in Cherokee. I found it odd then, as well as now, that the word tohi in Cherokee also means 'peace.' Gawonii taught me wellness and how to be at peace, but most importantly, he taught me how to live.

"Gawonii was held in high regard among the Cherokee and was very influential in their politics and their decisions. Even though he was never chief, most Cherokee felt he had tremendous influence within the tribe and possibly had more power than the actual chief, who was white. Our white chief was Will Thomas, whom I got to know well and had much respect for. Without Gawonii and Will Thomas as the Cherokee leaders, the eastern band of Cherokees would not have existed. They would have been relocated with the rest of the Cherokee to Oklahoma just ten years before I arrived. Many would have died walking the Trail of Tears.

"With Gawonii's soft manner of speech, his ability to reason, and his kind understanding and Will's legal knowledge and fortitude to argue a point, they could save the tribe and their land."

Samuel and I have been walking a dirt road for over an hour as he tells his story. We seem to be climbing higher and deeper into the mountains. My legs are burning with fatigue, and my stomach growls with hunger; my mouth is dry with thirst. Samuel seems to notice and smiles, saying, "Jonathan, it is time we rest. This just so happens to be my favorite spot." He waves me to his side as he strolls down to the tumbling creek beside the road.

I gladly recline in the shade along the bank of the creek. Samuel takes a leather pouch from his jacket pocket and unwraps four biscuits, each with a slice of salt-cured ham. He offers me two, which I accept with pleasure.

He takes the empty leather pouch and dips it into the cold mountain stream. He fills it with the ice-cold water and sets it between the two of us to drink from. I take my shoes and socks off and dangle my sore feet in the cold stream.

Samuel eats his biscuits slowly, savoring each bite as if it is an exotic delicacy. The more I learn of him, the less I seem to understand him. The more he tells of his life, the more questions I seem to have. I now ask him, "Tell me what it is you smoke in your pipe. I hope it tastes better than it smells."

Samuel laughs, and as if he were reminded, he takes out his corncob pipe and fills the bowl with the stringy tobacco. He says, "It's jimsonweed. Some call it locoweed. I think 'loco' is much more representative of its nature." And he lights the bowl and takes a deep draw. He continues with his explanation. "The smoking of loco was common among the Cherokee men. In the council house when the men would meet, the pipe would be passed. It was ceremonial in some respects, but it was also enjoyed. Loco has a mild hallucinatory affect. The Cherokee felt it allowed them to communicate with their spirits much more effectively. Would you like to try it?" And Samuel hands the pipe to me.

I hold the pipe, a little afraid, but I am too curious not to try it. I take a small puff, inhaling it deeply. I cough and expel the acrid smoke that filled my lungs, and it seems that part of my lungs comes out as well. Still coughing, I hand him the pipe back and say, "Heavens, Samuel, how does one enjoy that?"

We both laugh. Samuel continues smoking. I continue trying to imagine his life.

CHAPTER SIX

There are as many worlds as there are kinds of days, and as an opal changes its colors and its fire to match the nature of a day, so do I.

—John Steinbeck

Samuel informs me that we are to cross the stream at this point and continue our trek on a small path through the woods. We walk into the deep foliage of conifers and climb steeply up the side of the mountain. Samuel tells me we are now on Wa-ya.

The area we now walk appears to be more remote than anywhere I had ever been. The trail on which we walk is not much more than a game trail. At places the trail disappears altogether, and I hope that Samuel knows his way, for if we become lost, I have doubts if we would ever find our way back to civilization.

We walk a mile or two, and Samuel stops. He waves me to follow him into a tunnel of mountain laurel. I follow. We stroll into a clearing that is marked with oddly shaped boulders. Upon closer inspection, I realize the boulders are makeshift tombstones. I realize we were now walking among Samuel's adoptive ancestors.

Samuel walks quietly, reverently. He stops at one marker and kneels to study the inscription. He says, "This is where we buried Gawonii. My Cherokee father."

The inscription on the front of the boulder is barely visible. The stone itself is only mildly smooth on the face, and the inscription appears to be roughly hand chiseled. Samuel rubs the stone affectionately, perhaps a ceremonial act. Samuel says, "Gawonii lived to be quite old in his human life. I was fortunate to have spent many years by his side. I grew to love him as a father, and he grew to love me as a son. I miss him terribly."

Samuel then struggles to his feet and moves to the next stone. At this one he drops to his knees as if in defeat and embraces the stone. He weeps uncontrollably. In anguish, I watch my friend Samuel.

Samuel regains his composure and says, "Jonathan. This is where I buried my brother Peter."

I step beside Samuel and put my arm around his shoulders in hopes of giving my friend some comfort. He speaks to Peter's grave as if he is talking to his old friend. "My dear Degataga, I have found the bugle that seemed to be your torment. I have removed it from our life forever. I hope you no longer hear its taunting."

We both stand there for a moment or two more before Samuel once again moves further among the small boulders. He stops at several of the markers and takes a moment to reflect, but at most of them, he doesn't bother to tell me who the ancestor was or what the significance is. I could tell by Samuel's reaction to each marker how significant the relationship had been.

He kneels once again at one small stone. He touches the stone and mumbles something quietly, not wanting me to hear what he has said. He then turns to me and says, "This is where we buried

Ahyoka. She was the love of my life." A tear drifts down Samuel's cheek, and his lips quiver with sorrow.

I look at Samuel and say, "She was your wife?"

"No, Jonathan. She was Cherokee, and I was negro. Even the Cherokee with their great understanding of life could not allow a negro to marry one of their own. That was the law; that was the way it was."

"Ahyoka? What does that mean in Cherokee?"

"She brought happiness. That is what it means."

"Samuel, that seems so unfair. So sad. So you never married? Never married anyone?"

Samuel shakes his head and says, "If I could not marry Ahyoka, I would marry no one."

I ask Samuel, "And what happened to her? How did she die?"

"Gawonii said she died from a broken heart."

I look at Samuel and think how unfair it seemed to deny him the right to marry Ahyoka. Why could not the Cherokee accept him as one of their own and allow them to wed? How it must torment him just as the bugle had tormented Peter.

I say, "It seems so unfair."

Samuel smiles and says, "As I said, Peter was the only one that ever accepted me as an equal. Even the Cherokee had laws that prevented me from ever being an equal. I could never own or carry a weapon. That was the law. I could never marry outside of my race. That was the law as well. As unjust as it seems, I understood then, as I do now."

I let Samuel stroll among his ancestors in quiet reverence. I watch as he pays his respects to the many who had touched his life in different ways. I wonder to myself how it must feel to witness the passing of so many lives that had mattered. It is no wonder he does not count his sorrows.

We once again begin to walk, and Samuel resumes his story.

"It was not as bad as you would think, Jonathan. The Cherokee were a very civilized people. They had great patience with me. They taught me their language, and most importantly, they taught me to live as they did.

"The Cherokee, contrary to what most think, were farmers. They had small plots of land where they farmed squash, corn, and a variety of beans. They had cattle, pigs, and chickens. There always seemed to be an abundance of food. Any excess they would sell to the white townships, and with the profits they would buy tools and clothes and anything else they could not manufacture themselves. They were quite ingenious. The chief, Will Thomas, became quite successful, and he began buying land that he allowed the Cherokee to call their own. The Cherokee felt that land could never be owned. The land was everyone's, and it was everyone's responsibility to protect and respect it. The whites felt that if there was no deed to the land, then they had the free right to call it their own—which they did with vigor until Will Thomas began to protect the Cherokee's interest. Gawonii convinced the Cherokee, and Will Thomas convinced the whites, that they could work together and live in harmony. It worked well."

I nod and question him. "And you, Samuel—what did you do for the Cherokee?"

Samuel shrugs his shoulders and says, "I taught them to fish and showed them new ways to farm. They were unfamiliar with the process of rotating crops and the use of fertilizer and for years were unwilling to fence any property. Their cattle and pigs roamed the countryside with no care. If a cow or a pig roamed onto a white's property, the white would claim it as their own. Using locust rails, I showed them how to fence and rotate the pastures as well. My ideas were well received and seemed to work."

I question once again, "And Peter? What did he do?"

Samuel smiles and says, "He was being groomed to take Gawonii's place as the didanawisgi, the medicine man. He was very good. I took great pleasure in watching Peter learn from Gawonii. They both seemed to share the same spirit. I was proud of my brother Peter."

I look at Samuel and decide to press further, seeking more information about Peter. "And did Peter become didanawisgi, the medicine man?"

Samuel gives a sorrowful look and shakes his head no. Judging his reaction to the question, I choose not to push with that line of questioning any further. At least for now.

"Tell me about how the Cherokee and the whites got along. You implied there may have been some disputes between them."

"Yes, there were many disputes. The whites could not understand the Cherokee way, and they tried to impose their will. The disputes usually involved land. The whites could not understand that the Cherokee only wanted to take from the land what they could use. The Cherokee farmed small plots, and there was very little waste. For instance, the corn we grew—the shucks, the leaves covering the corn, would be left on the ears of corn to supplement the nutrient value of the dried corn. Some of the corn was ground into cornmeal; some corn would be shelled off the cob to feed the chickens and to fatten the hogs. The shucks were fed to the cows and horses to supplement their diet of hay. We would even pull the fodder, the leaves on the cornstalks themselves, and these would be used to feed the livestock as well. Nothing was wasted, and nothing was grown and harvested that was more than what our people needed."

I look at Samuel, and I can tell he is enjoying the talk of farming and the Cherokee way. He seems proud.

We walk into a heavily forested cove. The forest floor is covered with fallen timber, decaying and covered in emerald-green moss. Large green ferns sprout in abundance on both sides of the small trail where we walk. We approach a tiny stream that tumbles down the mountainside.

Samuel turns to the right off the trail, and I follow him. We climb a short hill and arrive on a relatively flat plateau, beside which the stream cascades. There are a few logs and stacked stones littering the area. Samuel smiles and says, "This is where we had our village for many years."

I study the area and try to imagine what it would have been like to live so remotely. There were no roads, no grocery stores, no electricity, and no running water, other than the stream itself. I question Samuel. "How many homes were here at that time?"

Samuel responds, "There were as many as twelve homes at one time. Plus, we had the council house, which stood there." He points to several stacks of stone and logs lying about. He walks over to one side of the clearing and says, "Here is where Peter and I had our house."

The only remnants of Samuel and Peter's house are a short stack of stones that may have been a part of a foundation. There was nothing else.

We walk to the side where the creek crosses the plateau, and I see evidence of stone walls and terraced plots of land. The land that had once been cultivated and planted with corn and other vegetables now is overgrown with dog hobble and rhododendron.

Samuel confirms what I think. "This is where we grew our crops."

I nod that I understand and ask, "How long did you and the Cherokee live here? When did you move?"

Samuel walks over, sits on one of the terraced walls, and crosses his legs. He says, "Come sit, Jonathan. Let me tell you more of my story."

CHAPTER SEVEN

Only in the darkness can you see the stars.

—Martin Luther King Jr.

Samuel begins telling more of his story.

"I was adopted into the Cherokee in 1853. It was quite ceremonial. All the men gathered in the council, and I was adopted into the tribe. It was *a ni wo di,* or 'paint clan.' The a ni wo di clan were known as the medicine people. Of course, I didn't know that then. In your terms, this group or clan of Cherokee would be considered a very spiritual group, in harmony with nature and the spirits of the natural world.

"The ceremony lasted most of the night. The men smoked the pipe, and I did as well. Each attendee spoke either for me or against me. There was quite a discussion about the fact that I had been a slave. The Cherokee were sensitive to this. It was a controversial topic for the group. Some felt slavery was acceptable, and some felt it was reprehensible. I enjoyed listening to each speak their minds, but I was growing anxious as to what might be my eventuality.

"Gawonii spoke eloquently. With his soft-spoken word and his keen sense of wisdom, he won the group over to his thinking. Much of the discussion was in Cherokee, which I did not understand, and I could only observe their demeanor as to what my outcome might be. As the night came to an end and the assembled group seemed to come to an agreement, Gawonii began to cry. He waved me to his side and hugged me—as tight a hug as I have ever received. He said to me in English, 'Welcome, son. You are now a ni wo di.

"Everyone in the group hugged me and seemed to accept me without penitence. I felt at that moment as if I was accepted, but I was soon to find out that I only had limited rights.

"I was a negro, and I could never have a weapon in my possession. I could never marry outside of my race. I had no rights to their oral stories, no rights to traditional medicine, no rights to inherit medicine men's names without family approval, no rights to speak for any tribal nations, and no rights to vote in tribal elections, yet I still felt for once in my life that I was a part of a nation. I felt I had the freedom to act within that nation. I felt free!

"Jonathan, it is hard for me to explain the feeling I felt. To be a slave, and then to be welcomed into this group of Cherokees. To become an active part of their community, to be asked my opinion, and to be accepted almost as their equal was astounding to me. I wished my mother had been there. I was free, but not yet equal.

"It was only a few days after I was adopted into the a ni wo di that I met Ahyoka. She was the most beautiful girl I think I had ever seen. She had long, flowing black hair. She was tall and thin and had the smile of an angel. I think I fell in love with her the first time I saw her. She smiled at me when she first saw me. I think maybe I was an oddity to her. I was black and not dressed as they were, and I did not speak their language. Peter introduced me as his brother, and she seemed immediately enchanted.

"I came to realize that Gawonii and Peter were considered the elite of the clan, and so I was as well.

"Peter and I hunted, farmed, and played as young teens did, but I also spent moments with Ahyoka. Peter would spend hours teaching me the Cherokee language, and when he tired, Ahyoka was there to help. The three of us became inseparable. I loved Peter as a brother, but I began to love Ahyoka in a way that was unfamiliar.

"Two years or more went by, and I had solidified my position within a ni wo di. I was happy, and the tribe was doing well. The law of the land was that negroes should not be taught to read or write, but the Cherokee had insisted they were separate. Even though they were not all in agreement, they began teaching their adopted negroes to read and write, both in Cherokee and English. I dedicated most of my time to learn what they were willing to teach. With Ahyoka's and Peter's help, by the end of my two years of freedom, I was proficient in both Cherokee and English and could read and write both rather well.

"I learned from Gawonii much of the history of the Cherokee people and their beliefs. I found their ideas, their interpretations of life, strange and foreign, but I slowly began to accept them as my beliefs as well. Gawonii told me not long after I was adopted of how disease and sickness had almost decimated his people over the years, and he told me why. Gawonii told me in the beginning of this world when life was new, all manner of new creatures came into this world. There was *awi,* the deer; *yvna,* the bear; *tsista,* the rabbit; *giihlithe,* the dog; *suli,* the buzzard; and many others. Last of the creatures born was a strange new animal called man.

"In those days, every living thing could communicate with one another because they spoke a common language. People could talk to animals or the water, the plants, the fire, or the stones. All beings respected and understood each other and took only what each needed to live. But gradually within man, something began to change.

"People forgot they were a part of one Great Life. They neglected to maintain a harmonious way of being (*duyukta*). They would take more than they needed and showed disrespect for other creatures. Instead of taking one deer, they would kill an entire herd, taking only the choice meat and leaving the rest to rot. They poisoned whole pools of fish instead of catching a few. They trampled insects and other small creatures through dislike or carelessness.

"As people continued to separate themselves from the rest of the Great Life and disregard the laws of nature, they forgot how to speak the original language.

"When the animal nations came together in council, they would ask, 'What do we do about the problem of man?' The bear nation held a council, and the Great White Bear asked his people this question. Their answer was to declare war on man.

"The Great White Bear realized that men were much too numerous and aggressive to defeat, and he convinced the bears to not wage war on man for fear of their own defeat.

"Over the years, other animal nations held their councils, but they too could come to no conclusion what to do about the problem of man.

"Finally, the creeping, crawling nation—the insects—held a council, and they decided to give man disease. As they shouted out the names of each disease—liver disease, heart disease, pain in the joints, fever—these illnesses came into the world. Every man, woman, and child was afflicted, and many died, but a few began to recover.

"So to rid themselves of man completely, the chief of the insects, the White Grubworm, went to the chief of the Green People, Grandfather Ginseng (*yvwi usdi*). He asked Grandfather Ginseng to help the insects destroy mankind.

"The plants are a patient people, and the ginseng plant asked for four days to pray and think about the decision. After four days, Grandfather Ginseng said, 'We have heard your words, and there is much truth in them. People have hurt and abused us as much or more than they have you. But we also understand that man is still young and foolish, and we are all part of the same Great Life. So we have decided that if people come to us in a good way, a sacred way, we will help them by giving them the cure for every disease which you, the insects, have made.

"This is a promise made to us by the Green People, and to this day, they honor their pledge by providing us with food and medicine. It is still a common practice among Cherokee herbalists to walk through the woods allowing the needed medicine to announce itself by unusual shaking or other obvious signs.

"Gawonii taught me things like this.

"It was about this time when I first met Will Thomas. He was a white man but also the chief of the Cherokee. Gawonii introduced me to him when Thomas came to visit one day. Gawonii told him the story of how I had come to be a part of the clan and how I had helped them progress with their farming techniques.

"Will Thomas seemed to be impressed and had me show him the plots of land we had farmed and how well they seemed to produce. He was impressed. He was much older than I, possibly the age of Gawonii, but Will was wiser than the Cherokee and was surely wiser than me. He questioned me about the rotation of crops and the fencing. He seemed most interested in our fertilizing process and in the end seemed very intrigued. He wanted me to come to Qualla town to help his community prosper as ours had in farming. I agreed with the stipulation that I could bring Peter.

"Will Thomas smiled, shook my hand, and said, 'Samuel, bring whomever you want. You are what we need.'

"Peter and I decided to move to Qualla town, which was forty miles north. We packed our belongings, which were few, and loaded them onto two mules given to us by Gawonii. We began our journey north into an area called the Nantahala.

"Nantahala means 'land of the noonday sun' in Cherokee, and I soon discovered why. The mountains create a gorge for at least fifteen miles. A huge, cascading river tumbles through the gorge, and with the height of the mountains on either side, one cannot see the sun except at noonday. It is a most beautiful sight to see but also the most unlivable. Peter and I traveled for four days before arriving at the Oconaluftee River, where the township of Qualla was located.

"Qualla was much larger than where we had lived and the farmland much more abundant. Peter and I were given a small stone house, and we began teaching the fundamentals of farming to the *a ni gi lo hi* clan.

"I found it most fulfilling to improve their livelihood.

"Will Thomas and I spoke on several occasions, not about farming or my being a negro, but about the issue of slavery. He seemed most concerned.

"He explained that the country was soon going to come to a dilemma of deciding for slavery or against it, and the Cherokee would have to decide as well. I told Will about the horrors I had witnessed and vowed I would never accede to any idealization of slavery.

"Will Thomas told me that as a tribe of the South, we must support the Southern ideals, for if there was ever a war, a civil war, we would be at the mercy of the South if they were to succeed.

"With Thomas's wisdom and his gentle explanation, I began to realize that maybe he was right. Neither of us was for slavery, but standing against the possible secession from the North's federalism was a desirable tactic.

"I taught Will Thomas and the people of Qualla how to farm, and Will Thomas taught me how to think as a politician. He taught me how to seek my freedom in a completely different way than I had ever imagined. I once again began to feel freer.

"After a year or so, Peter and I packed our belongings once again and headed south, back to our home at Wa-ya.

"I was excited about going back. I wanted to see Ahyoka. I had missed her. I wanted to see Gawonii and seek his wisdom on what I had learned from Will Thomas. I wanted to spend more time with my brother, Peter, hunting and fishing as we had done in the past. For the first time in my life, I was homesick.

"We traveled back through the Nantahala gorge and into the area of Wa-ya. Within only a year, the whites had settled much more densely than I would have thought in the areas around Wa-ya and even in the gorge itself.

"Peter and I would get strange looks as we led our mules through the small townships of whites. Some would be offensive, calling out 'Nigger!' as we passed. On several occasions, Peter would take offense and confront the offenders and back them down with his brawn.

"I would tell Peter to not bother defending me. I was free; that was all I wanted to be.

"Peter saw me as an older brother, a brother he admired, a brother he loved. He saw no color. I admired him to overlook our obvious differences; we were not the same. He was Cherokee, and I was...something else.

"We arrived at Wa-ya and were welcomed with cheers!

"Gawonii seemed most interested in the discussions I had with Will Thomas about slavery, and we spent many days discussing slavery and where the Cherokee should stand on the matter.

"Our discussions concerning slavery were sparked once again in 1857, when the Supreme Court ruled and said that Congress did not have the right to ban slavery in the States and that furthermore, slaves were not citizens.

"It was during 1857 and 1860 that Gawonii, Peter, and I traveled once again to Qualla town upon Will Thomas's request to discuss and help formulate a plan for the Cherokee if North Carolina chose to secede from the union.

"The council house was filled with leaders of the Cherokee and several white politicians from the capital city of Raleigh. The discussions were most heated, with many of the Cherokee siding with the North and stating their hatred and distaste for slavery as the reason. Many of the white politicians took issue, stating that the Constitution gave the state the power to decide whether they were to be a free state or one of slavery, and they argued that the radical Republicans of the North were trying illegally to abolish slavery. The whites argued that North Carolina's economy depended primarily on agriculture, primarily cotton, and without the use of slaves, the economy would suffer greatly.

"During this time of heated discussions, I was introduced to a most interesting white man. As radical as some of the white politicians were for slavery, he was most outspoken against it. He was ready to take up arms against the government to abolish slavery. He inflamed the group so much that they threatened to imprison him, and I heard some even threaten to kill him. He was forced to leave—but not before he pleaded and tried to recruit the Cherokee to join his forces. His name was John Brown. A little over a year later, he staged an attack and captured the federal arsenal at Harpers Ferry, where he was eventually captured and hung.

"It was eventually decided that it would be in the Cherokees' best interest to align themselves with the Confederates if the Southern states chose to secede. When Abraham Lincoln was elected in 1860, we knew the South was readying themselves for war, and in 1861 at Park Hill, the Cherokee nation signed a treaty with the Confederate government.

"Gawonii, Peter, and I returned to Wa-ya and prepared our small village for the possibility of war."

CHAPTER EIGHT

Being deeply loved by someone gives you strength, while loving someone deeply gives you courage.

—Lao Tzu

I listen to Samuel's story with intense interest. I know many of the historical happenings he speaks of. I know of John Brown and Harpers Ferry. I have studied in detail the historical events leading up to the Civil War, but to hear it from someone who has witnessed it personally is particularly moving.

Samuel stands, pats me on the shoulder, and says, "I hope I'm not boring you with my story."

"Not at all, Samuel. I find it most interesting. Please, continue telling me more."

Samuel studies me for a moment and grins. He says, "Let's head back to Glen Choga. It is getting late."

We walk side by side back down the mountain and cross the stream once again. Samuel continues telling me more of his story.

"Our village on Wa-ya was very remote, as you have seen. Gawonii felt we would probably be able to ride out the war without any harm or interference from either the Confederates or the Union. There was no one from our village that joined the Confederacy, although Qualla village had several Cherokee that fought with the Confederates. Most ended up losing their lives in the first few battles they were a part of.

"Peter, Ahyoka, and I pretty much continued with our lives as if the war did not exist. Occasionally we could hear skirmishes way off in the distance, but only rarely did we see any soldiers.

"Ahyoka and I began to spend more and more time together. It may have been the threat of the war and not knowing what the future might bring, but we were falling in love.

"Ahyoka wanted me to tell her what being a slave was like, and when I told her, she wept uncontrollably. She was horrified that people were treated in that manner. I wished I had not told her the truth, for it must have affected the faith she had in man for her eternity.

"She told me what it was like being raised as a Cherokee. She described the fear in the clan when the Cherokee were being imprisoned, collected, and removed to Oklahoma. She described the horror with such detail that I felt her life may have not been much better than mine.

"Ahyoka means 'She brings happiness' in Cherokee, and I must say she brought me much happiness. She taught me to understand the spirit, the balance of nature in all living things.

"I had come to Wa-ya ten years past and had known Ahyoka for the same. She was the most beautiful girl I think I had ever seen; but it was her spirit—her soul—that I fell in love with. She taught me to look deep into the soul—not only hers, but of every living creature. She taught me how to love, and I will always be indebted to her for that gift.

"I was twenty-five years old and had never felt that kind of love before. She loved me deeply, and I loved her as well, but Gawonii in all his wisdom saw what was beginning to happen. He called me to his house, and we smoked the pipe. He questioned me about my feelings for Ahyoka and what my intentions were. I told him that I loved her beyond belief and I knew she loved me.

"Gawonii explained that I had used bad judgment and allowed a relationship to form that should not have been. He described it as a tragedy to allow two hearts to wander down a path that would end in sorrow.

"I begged Gawonii for his approval to marry Ahyoka. He listened to my reasoning as I tried to explain. I saw in Gawonii's eyes that day the sorrow I brought upon him. I had placed him in a position where he could not win. If he refused the marriage, then he would have broken my heart; he loved me deeply. But if he allowed the marriage, then he would have gone against the Cherokee way, and he loved that even more.

"Gawonii hugged me tightly and wept before refusing the marriage between myself and Ahyoka. He held me in his arms, and I wept as well.

"The refusal of the marriage eventually ruined my and Ahyoka's friendship, for the pain we shared between us was too great to bear. Once there had been three. Peter, Ahyoka, and myself, friends that shared happy dreams for the future. Now there was only Peter and myself, looking back at my sorrow.

"Two years after the war had started, Peter was being groomed to be the didanawisgi, the medicine man, and I worked the plots of land. We still would fish, almost daily, and occasionally would go into the mountains to trap or hunt, although we stayed close to the village for fear of coming across either the Confederate or Union soldiers.

"That was when we happened upon the camp of Union soldiers at the pond. After that horrific battle scene, Peter was never the same. Our friendship remained, but he was so tormented by what he had witnessed, I thought he may go crazy.

"In 1864, there was a small detachment of Confederate soldiers that came into our village, escorted by Will Thomas from Qualla. They met with Gawonii for the better part of the day, and as the sun was beginning to set, they sent for Peter and me to join the group in the council house. I was terribly afraid at what may be in store for the two of us.

"They were enlisting the Cherokees' help to guide a small group of soldiers and two wagons of supplies across the mountains to the area of Savannah, Georgia. They described the supplies as being of extreme importance, but no other details were given.

"Gawonii was not given much choice to refuse the request made by the Confederates. He thought immediately of me, since I had traveled that route about ten years before as a young slave. We were to take the most remote of routes in hopes of avoiding any contact with the enemy.

"The route we were to take was most difficult, even on foot, and was going to be nearly impossible with two wagons loaded down with supplies, but like Gawonii, I had no choice but to agree. Peter and I prepared to escort the soldiers and wagons across the Appalachians and to the Savannah River.

"There were two wagons of supplies and a detachment of twelve soldiers. There were two officers that were on horseback, and the rest of the soldiers were without. The wagons were heavy with supplies, and they were pulled by two oxen each. We began our journey from Qualla town.

"We traveled back through the gorge of Nantahala and into the area of Wa-ya, passing very close to our village. We followed close to the same route I had taken ten years before.

"The soldiers we traveled with were battle weary, and the officers maintained very little discipline. I thought that many would probably desert before ever reaching Savannah. I felt the mission was foolhardy.

"Peter and I kept our distance from the soldiers, choosing to sleep away from their rowdy behavior, and we only conversed with them when the need arose. The soldiers would drink themselves into a stupor many nights, and I feared that if we came upon the enemy that these soldiers with whom we traveled would be no match for even the most inexperienced.

"We were in the area just west of Yunwitsule-nunyi, where I had hidden in the caves for months before coming to live with the Cherokee. I knew the area well and was surprised to come upon a small village of Cherokee. It was late in the day when we passed through, and the soldiers insisted we camp at the village. The Cherokee were very hospitable to our group, realizing that Peter and I, the grandsons of Gawonii, were leading.

"I tried to convince the officers to travel farther, to gain the most distance for the day, but they would not listen. I was fearful of what may come of the village if the enemy discovered our group and even more fearful of what the rowdy soldiers may do themselves. The officers ordered Peter and I to take the wagons with one sentry well into the woods, where we were to stay till the next morning.

"We did as we were told, distancing ourselves almost a mile away from the village, and both Peter and I worried of what may result.

"During the middle of the night, we were awakened by gunfire. It was distant but in the direction of the village. Me, Peter, and the sentry set off at a trot to investigate. Upon our arrival at the village, the soldiers were drunken and were dragging the young women of the village about, raping them in front of their very homes. Several of the men of the village apparently had tried to intervene, and they lay dead amid the chaos.

"The rage I felt was sickening, and Peter had the same rage in his eyes as me. The young sentry with us noticed our anger and pointed his rifle at both of us, ready to shoot if we tried to intervene. With one quick swipe of Peter's knife, the young soldier was almost beheaded. Peter took the soldier's rifle and gave me the pistol, and without much thought or planning we ran into the village with such speed and hate that within five minutes, all eleven of the soldiers lay dead.

"The village was in disarray, but Peter and I convinced the village to never tell what happened there. We must make everyone believe that we came across the enemy and that the Confederates were all killed in the battle that ensued. Peter and I then went back to the wagons to decide what we must do with them.

"To our surprise, the wagons were filled with crates that contained hundreds, maybe even thousands, of gold bricks. We did not even bother to count the crates or bars. There was so much that counting it seemed impossible. Neither of us knew what to do.

"Neither of us slept that night. Instead, we discussed our options, and by morning we had decided to take the gold and hide it in a nearby cave that I knew.

"It was very difficult to move the wagons to the area where the cave was located. We had moved slowly throughout the day, and darkness fell on us quickly. We continued moving toward the cave.

"The wagon I was driving accidentally rolled one wheel into a large rut in the trail and became stuck. Peter, using a log as leverage, worked from behind the wagon as I coaxed the oxen trying to free the heavy wagon. I whipped the oxen, and Peter pushed and pulled from behind, and I thought we almost succeeded, but there was a crack, and the wagon fell to one side. Peter yelled with pain as the heavy wagon tilted and fell sideways upon him. The full weight of the wagon lay on the lower portion of both legs. He was screaming in pain, and I tried with all my might to free him, but it was no use. I unhooked the oxen and tried to use them to pull the wagon upright to free Peter from underneath, but that did not work either. The whole time, Peter was screaming in agony, and I did not know what to do.

"I worked the entire night, removing all the gold bars from the overturned wagon and tried to use the oxen to pull it upright. I tried digging him out from under the wagon, but nothing seemed to work. All the while, Peter screamed in agony.

"At daybreak, I lay beside my brother and cried, not knowing what else to do. Peter stared at me with eyes that had given up as well. He told me to take the pistol and to shoot him in the head and put him out of his misery and to do it quickly. He said I owed him that much if I loved him as he loved me.

"I killed my brother that day, and I have had to live with that pain ever since."

I glance at Samuel as he tells his story. There are tears that trickle from his eyes, and he dabs at them with the back of his hand. He seems fatigued, and I suggest we sit.

I said, "Samuel, you had no other choice. What you did was difficult, but it would have been much worse to allow him to die slowly. You did the right thing."

Samuel just nodded and said, "Gawonii once told me there is a battle between two wolves inside us all. One wolf is evil. It is anger, jealousy, greed, resentment, inferiority, lies, and ego. The other wolf is good. It is joy, peace, love, hope, humility, kindness, empathy, and truth. I asked Gawonii which wolf wins. And Gawonii quietly replied, the one you feed."

CHAPTER NINE

We must embrace pain and burn it as fuel for our journey.

—Kenji Miyazawa

Samuel and I walk slowly back to the lodge and arrive a little after dark. Samuel suggests I eat with the other guests; he is tired and feels he may just have his dinner brought to his room.

I nod yes, thinking Samuel needs a little time away from recounting the horrific stories of his past.

Samuel retires to his room. Thomas and I have dinner in the dining room.

Thomas is in a jovial mood, and right away, I feel I want to escape from him, for I am in no mood for his lightheartedness. I choose to drink whiskey, and after the second one, the sadness and sorrow that had overwhelmed me earlier seem to disappear.

I stay up late with Thomas, drinking whiskey and telling him of my wild escapades when I attended Harvard. We both laugh, and I begin to forget the horror stories that had been told to me earlier that day.

I am afraid to go to my room and try to sleep, for I fear the horror will fill me and create such horrific nightmares that I may never sleep normally again. I stay and sip my whiskey till everyone leaves and then surrender and go to my room, fearful of the night that I might endure.

It may be due to the excessive amount of whiskey I had or the miles I walked, but once I lie down on my bed, I fall asleep immediately. There are no nightmares that plague me. I sleep till well after sunrise the next morning.

I eat breakfast alone. Thomas is sleeping even later than I, and for some reason, I am avoiding Samuel. This concerns me, for I am intrigued by his story and have grown very fond of the old man, but his story at times is so troubling that I'm unable to sort the emotions—his emotions as well as mine.

I go to Alexander, the proprietor, and ask if I may use the phone to call my boss in New York.

Anna, Sims's secretary, answers and then connects me. "Hello, Harold. Jonathan here. Just wanted to let you know things are progressing well with the story on Samuel Timmons. I have spent the better part of three days in interviews, and the photographer has captured some tremendous photos. I think you will find the story quite interesting. I should be able to wrap this up in another day or so."

Harold is quiet on the other end of the phone and then replies. "Oh! Yes, Jonathan. Yes, Samuel Timmons. I remember now. Of course, if it takes another day or so, that is fine. Glad to hear things are going well. Call me when you are finished."

Harold hangs up, and I stand there with the phone in my hand, feeling rejected and worthless. I have a fear that maybe I do not have the talent or skill to write Samuel's story in the way that it deserves. I fear I may not be able to capture the emotions, the sorrows, and the joys that he expresses with such eloquence.

I walk outside to find Samuel.

I find him sitting beneath a grouping of tall hemlocks close to the pond. He is smoking his pipe and building something from small branches and cord. I say to him, "Good morning, Samuel. I am so sorry I did not get up early to see you. I found myself rather tired."

Samuel smiles and says, "I was rather tired myself. I am making you something, Jonathan."

"What are you making, Samuel?"

"A dream catcher. When I finish, it will be quite elaborate. Do you know what a dream catcher is?"

"I'm afraid I do not," I say, and Samuel smiles again and begins to explain.

"Dreams are messages from sacred spirits. We must be attuned to them, but at times, bad dreams from evil spirits are sent, and they can affect our tohi. Do you remember what tohi is, Jonathan?"

"Yes. It means wellness or peace."

Samuel smiles and nods yes. He finishes the dream catcher by tying three feathers to it. He hands it to me proudly and says, "The hole in the middle here is for the good messages to pass through to your soul, and the bad messages from evil spirits will be trapped here and discarded when you wake. Your tohi will now be protected. Hang this above your bed when you sleep."

"Thank you very much, Samuel. It is very kind of you to give me this. I will keep it above my bed when I sleep."

We sit side by side, and I question Samuel. "The wagons full of gold. Whatever happened to the gold?"

Samuel begins to tell more of his story.

"I hid all the gold in a cave. The cave was so remote that I knew no one would ever find it. I later discovered that all that gold was from the Confederate treasury. It had been stored in Montgomery for most of the war, but when the Union began to capture much of the South, the Confederates devised a plan to move it to Savannah. There, they would ship it to France, preventing the Union from confiscating it. The Confederates planned to use the gold to help finance the war.

"It was a lot of gold, Jonathan, and I could not tell anyone about it. I could not even tell Gawonii, for I feared I may be hung for my part in the killing of the Confederate soldiers.

"I turned the oxen loose and left the empty wagons where they were. It took me three days to eventually free Peter's body from beneath the turned-over wagon. I took one of the horses of the dead Confederates and carried his body back to Wa-ya to be buried.

"I told Gawonii and Will Thomas that our party had been bushwhacked by a large detachment of Union soldiers and that all were killed except for myself. I explained that I hid in the woods after the battle until the Union soldiers were gone. I explained that when I eventually found the wagons, they had been emptied.

"Both Gawonii and Will Thomas accepted my explanation without any suspicion. Neither of them seemed to be aware of the actual contents of the wagon.

"After the war, slavery was abolished, but the freed slaves had nothing and nowhere to go. It was not as good as one would think. In the South, whites dominated the legislature, and 'black codes' were passed to limit the movement and labor practices. Even though the slaves had been emancipated, their freedom was restricted greatly.

"It was two years after the war when I decided to travel back to Edgefield to find my mother. I discovered she had moved to Charleston, where there seemed to be more promise of employment. I went there in hopes of finding her.

"I was having difficulty in getting any information on the whereabouts of my mother, and my plight came to the notice of Joseph Rainey, a negro who was a state senator of South Carolina.

"Rainey and I had a lot in common. There was not much difference in age, and we both had been born into slavery. He had been given his freedom from slavery, and I had escaped slavery, both at a young age. He was one of the few that could influence and promote equal rights for the colored in the state of South Carolina and later in the US Congress. Rainey dedicated himself to helping me find my mother.

"Six months after arriving in Charleston and gaining Rainey's help, I discovered my mother had died not long after she arrived in Charleston. From what I was told, she had taken ill. A severe fever consumed her, and she had died. I was taken to the cemetery where she had been buried, and I found her marker. It was one of the saddest moments of my life. I was saddened that I never got to thank her for allowing my freedom.

"I felt indebted to Joseph Rainey for helping me find my mother. We became good friends, and he convinced me to stay on in Charleston to help him with his political affairs.

"Joseph got elected to the US Congress that year, and I worked for him to lend support for his efforts to gain equal rights for the colored.

"Rainey was the first person I helped finance with the gold. It was done in small amounts, and no one ever seemed to care how I came to have the gold. Over the years, there were many more I helped finance. There was Robert Smalls, Samuel McElwee, Robert Elliott, and many others. They were all black leaders who worked toward equal rights for the colored.

"In 1871, Joseph got three bills passed by Congress; they became known as the Force Acts. These three bills gave coloreds the right to vote, to hold office, to serve on juries, and to receive equal protection of laws.

"I helped finance efforts to bring colored people equal rights, and I did so with the gold from the Confederate treasury. I don't want you to think I used any of the gold for my personal use. I would have found that somewhat immoral, but I found a lot of satisfaction in using the gold of the Confederates to bring some justice for my people.

"It was around 1872 when I traveled with Joseph Rainey to Washington, DC, where I had the opportunity to meet the president of the United States, Ulysses S. Grant. President Grant enlisted Joseph's advice in developing strategies in the reconstruction of the South. It was upon Joseph's advice that President Grant began seeking advice from me as well. Immediately following the war, the South was very turbulent. Grant stabilized the nation during the turbulent Reconstruction period, prosecuted the Ku Klux Klan, and enforced civil and voting rights laws using the army and the department of justice.

"After President Grant heard my story and realized that not only had I been a slave but that I was also a Cherokee, he was quite intrigued and discussed with me on several occasions the problems with the Indians in the American West. Initially, his Indian peace policy was successful in reducing the violence in the West, and I took great satisfaction that I may have influenced this somewhat.

"On one occasion, he had summoned me to the White House. He wanted me to meet a lieutenant colonel who was being dispatched to help bring peace with the Indians in the West.

"I met with the colonel and discussed my experiences as a Cherokee. I told him of the injustices the Cherokee had dealt with, and I tried to reason with him that peace would only occur through understanding. War with the Indians would only create more separation and no lasting peace. I thought he listened to my advice, but I later found out that in 1876, he and all his men were killed in a battle at Little Bighorn. His name was Lieutenant Colonel George Armstrong Custer.

"I felt I had failed my Indian brothers in the West, so in 1877, I decided to return to my Cherokee home and help them as I had the colored."

Samuel and I decide to have dinner together once again. We sit on the back porch as we had done a couple of nights before, and we sip our wine and eat our dinner. I am curious as to Samuel's opinion of the American Indian War and whether he thinks it could have been avoided.

Samuel explains, "I cannot speak for the Lakota, Cheyenne, and Arapaho. I can only speak as a Cherokee, but I will say that the Cherokee believe very strongly in 'an eye for an eye and a tooth for a tooth.' The Cherokee never killed to win; they would kill only for retribution. If the enemy took one life, then the Cherokee would take one life of theirs. Even that seems rather barbaric to me, but once you realize that many cultures kill and go to war simply for monetary gain or to acquire more land, then in comparison, the Cherokee way seems somewhat civilized. The only way the war in the West could have been prevented was for the whites to seek peace through understanding. This is the same thing I had tried to explain to Colonel Custer."

I begin to understand Samuel's reasoning concerning the American Indian War, and I realize that this same reasoning was what he had tried to explain to me a couple of nights before concerning the war in Europe.

I feel extremely tired, even though we had not walked that day. I promise Samuel I would be up at sunrise the next morning and would meet him on the front porch. I say, "Good night, Samuel. I very much enjoyed our discussion today. I'll see you in the morning."

I turn down the covers of my bed and lie there thinking about the story I had been told. I find it hard to believe. I hang my dream catcher on the wall above my bed and fall asleep, feeling at peace.

CHAPTER TEN

Love her all your days, if you choose, but don't let it spoil you, for it's wicked to throw away so many good gifts because you can't have the one you want.

—Louisa May Alcott

I am up before sunrise and go to the dining room to have a cup of coffee. There is no one else there, and I read a Franklin newspaper over my coffee. I find it hard to critique their writings because my mind keeps wandering to Samuel and his story. I feel I have so many questions for him, but I would rather have him relate his story the way he sees fit.

I see Samuel walk to his normal rocker on the front porch. I take my coffee and join him. I say, "Good morning, Samuel. I hope you slept as well as me."

"Yes, Jonathan, I slept very well. I am glad the dream catcher worked for you." And he smiles kindly.

"Are we to walk today?" I ask him.

"If you like, we can, but I had planned to take you to Qualla town. I would like for you to see my home. If we go to Qualla town, we would need to take your automobile, for it is quite far to walk."

"Yes, Samuel. I would very much like to see your home and would be more than happy to use my automobile. I'm rather relieved to know that we will not be walking. My shoes do not have much sole left, I'm afraid." I laugh, as does Samuel.

As we drive the thirty to forty miles to Qualla town, I can't refrain from asking Samuel a few questions. I ask, "Samuel, you mentioned Joseph Rainey, the congressman that helped you find your mother, and how he worked to obtain civil rights for the colored. There were others you mentioned as well. Of those, which seemed to be the most successful in their endeavors?"

Samuel thought a minute and then said, "They were all successful in their own way, but the one that probably impressed me the most was Frederick Douglass. He was probably the wisest man I had ever met. He spoke with such eloquence and wisdom that everyone took notice. Even the whites listened. Many of his thoughts and sayings I still hold dear. He told me once about how he escaped slavery, and he told me, 'No man can put a chain about the ankle of his fellow man without at last finding the other end fastened about his own neck.' I thought that was a very wise observation."

I say, "Samuel, after you came back to your Cherokee home, had much changed?"

"Gawonii was still alive and doing well, and Will Thomas was still the chief. The Cherokee law had changed in 1875 to allow whites as well as colored people to marry within the Cherokee. I had learned this while in Washington and was quite anxious to return to Ahyoka. I was sure Gawonii would give me his blessing and allow us to wed. I was saddened to find that Ahyoka had died just the year before. She died of yellow fever. I had never been as saddened as when I learned this. Even discovering the death of my mother did not affect me as the death of my beautiful Ahyoka. I felt my own life had come to an end."

"That is so terrible, Samuel. I can't imagine any human enduring the pain and sorrow you have been dealt."

"I cried for days over the loss of Ahyoka, and I changed during that time. I knew I would never be the Samuel I once was."

Samuel tells me where to turn and gives me tidbits of information as we pass certain landmarks. He tells me, "That is the Nantahala River. That church was the first built in the gorge. There was where the general store stood." The information comes in abundance, and I listen with interest.

I question Samuel. "This town, Qualla, where you live now and where Will Thomas had lived—what does Qualla mean?"

Samuel says, "It means 'old woman.' Not sure which old woman it refers to, but I should explain that women had tremendous influence in the tribe's government and the tribe's decisions. Most clans were maternalistic; villages and clans solidified around the mothers of the clan, not the fathers."

I think that odd and ask myself why, but I don't question him about Cherokee women and their influence. With Samuel's instruction, I turn down a long gravel drive. There are several small, wood-framed houses along the drive. There are small plots of land dedicated to the planting of corn and beans beside each house. A few cattle dot green pastures behind the small houses, and again I see smoke wisp from stone chimneys, but I see no one in the fields.

Samuel smiles and says, "Turn in here. This is my home."

The house is like most of the others. It is a wood-framed house with a tin roof. It is white, as are the others along the road, and his house has a small vegetable garden as well. I find the house very unpretentious and wonder why someone who has lived his life rubbing elbows with the rich and famous lived in such an ordinary way.

I park in front of Samuel's house, and we walk onto his small front porch. There are two rockers that sit on the front porch, but Samuel opens his front door and begs me to come in. He is smiling broadly as we enter, and I can tell he is proud to show me his home. I nod and say, "Very beautiful home, Samuel. It seems very comfortable."

Samuel offers me a chair, and he lights a cast-iron, wood-burning stove at one end of the small room. He chooses a rocker next to mine and lights his corncob pipe. He reaches to a small side table beside his rocker and hands me a photo album. He smiles once again.

I open the album, and I see photographs in various sizes pasted to the pages. I see photographs that are wrinkled, cracked, and faded from age, each with captivating images. There are several pictures of a young Samuel, maybe thirty years of age. I see one of him and a smiling President Grant, shaking hands.

I can't stop thumbing through the photo album. I recognize Samuel in most of the photographs, but I can't help but wonder who the others are. I begin to question Samuel about each. I find myself pointing to a photo and saying, "Samuel, who is this standing with you? Is that who I think it is?" My questions come one after the other, and he tries to pacify me with short, to-the-point answers, but it just compels me to ask more questions.

Samuel proudly shows his photos and begins to tell me more of his story.

"I returned to Wa-ya around 1876. I was in my early thirties and had done quite well financially. Working with Rainey, Frederick Douglass, and many others enabled me to operate within their institutions. I worked hard for these men, and they compensated me well for my efforts.

"Gawonii was in poor health when I returned to Wa-ya, and he insisted that he spend what little time he had left teaching me to be didanawisgi, the medicine man. This is the only picture I have of Gawonii. He died about five years after this picture was taken. He was terribly upset to tell me of Ahyoka's death and was guilt ridden by the fact that he had not allowed us to wed years before.

"He told me that when Ahyoka took ill, she had given him a box full of her writings. There were letters, poems, and general prose that she had penned. She had told him to be sure to save them for me, for she wanted me to know how much her heart was always with me."

I take a few of the writings and begin to read. They are so touching that I find myself beginning to cry. Her writings explain very beautifully her love for Samuel and speak of the terrible pain she endured knowing she would never be with him.

I read three or four of her poems and a couple of her letters and cannot bring myself to read more, for my emotions are too exhausted. I hand the box back to Samuel who places the papers back in the box very carefully. He places it beneath the end table where it had been previously.

Samuel smiles and says, "You see, Jonathan, she was very special. She did love me. I wished I could express the love I had for her as eloquently.

"As you see, I live very modestly. My personal belongings are no more than the simple farmer's next door. This is how I have always lived my life. I feel I have been very fortunate and blessed. I have chosen to use what wealth I have acquired personally in the same way I chose to use the Confederates' gold. I chose to invest in making lives better for the colored and the Cherokee people. This I have dedicated my entire life to.

"This photo is of my good friend Paul Dunbar, and that is me next to him. He was a brilliant writer. He wrote his first book *Oak and Ivy* around 1892. That was about the time I first met him. I had been following his writings and poetry in several black newspapers and was compelled to travel to Dayton, Ohio, to meet him. I discovered that this brilliant young man, a brilliant writer, could barely make ends meet. He was working as an elevator operator in Dayton, and he barely made enough to pay for the ink and paper he needed to produce his beautiful works of literature. I decided to help finance his efforts so that he could publish his second book, *Majors and Minors*, which received great reviews. He eventually became a very successful and influential writer.

"Paul Dunbar and I became very good friends. It was a few years after I first met Paul that he introduced me to two of his friends that had helped him when they had a printing business. They were about the same age as Paul and were now operating a bicycle shop in Dayton, close to where Paul worked as an elevator operator. What I found most interesting about the two were their dreams and their plans to build a flying machine.

"Their names were Orville and Wilbur Wright. I listened to their discussions and explanations of how a flying machine should be built. They explained the details of their machine with such enthusiasm that I too began to share the same enthusiasm as them.

"I spent several weeks in Dayton, and much of that time was spent listening to Orville and Wilbur explain their plans for their flying machine. They showed me detailed drawings and diagrams, and they had acquired an impressive amount of knowledge on the subject. What they had discovered was that getting a machine to fly was not difficult. What was difficult was to fly it in a controlled manner. That problem had not been solved by them—or, for that matter, by anyone else.

"The two brothers were becoming frustrated with their efforts. One afternoon we sat on their front porch with a myriad of drawings of wing design. They argued between themselves as to what might work and what would not. I listened to them argue, and I watched a bird, a robin, swoop down and land gracefully on the grass of their front lawn. The robin would take flight once again, darting in and out of the surrounding trees. It was an impressive exhibition of controlled flight. I then voiced my opinion. I told them to watch the birds. Watch how their wings tilt and how the bird banks into the turn. I told them to watch the robin—watch it closely and in detail. They would find their answer there.

"Just two years later, Wilbur contacted me in North Carolina. I arranged for them to come to the eastern shoreline of North Carolina to test their new design. I am quite proud to have been there when they successfully flew their machine at Kitty Hawk in 1903. Here is a picture of me and Wilbur in front of their machine. I was sixty-five years of age then.

"From 1890 to the early 1900s, I could help many people—men, women, and a variety of races and cultures—advance their individual efforts to bring equal rights to all. Even though I had invested thousands, maybe even millions, of dollars to champion the equal rights for all, the gold that remained in the cave was still staggering. It appeared that the pile had never been touched. I began to fear that I may die before I saw the rest of the gold used in a just manner. That's when I sought the advice of a dear friend who lived and worked in Alabama."

Samuel then points to a picture and continues explaining. "Here is his picture. His name was Booker T. Washington.

"With his help, I could set up a series of trust funds, which would keep funds available for those that worked to bring equal rights to all long after I was gone. It was only then that I felt my life's work somewhat complete.

"After Gawonii died, I was left to be didanawisgi of our tribe, which resided here in Qualla town. I felt a tremendous responsibility, even more than I had felt in all my efforts in the civil-rights movement. I think this was so because I knew I could never be as wise as my father Gawonii. I felt I was so inadequate.

"I remember Gawonii telling me that to be didanawisgi is not so much about wisdom but more about compassion. He said healing one is not about touching the other with your hands but touching them with your heart. I learned much from Gawonii, but the task seemed daunting all the same.

"What I discovered was that the teachings of Gawonii enabled me to understand and to bring peace—not only to the Cherokee but to all. What Gawonii taught me did not answer the problems of the world, for no one knows what the future might bring, but he taught me how to use my heart and how to bring wellness through compassion and understanding. It was quite liberating."

Samuel stands and walks to a window that looks out over the front lawn. He seems to be reminiscing silently, and I choose to let the silence stand.

Samuel continues to gaze beyond the window, and he asks me, "Jonathan. In your opinion, did I do right in using the Confederate gold? Should I have admitted killing those soldiers and suffered the consequences? I must say that in my whole life, that one thing is the only thing over which I still feel some regret."

I stand and walk over next to Samuel. I say, "I think it took an extreme amount of courage to do what you did. I personally admire your actions, but it is not for me to judge. God will be your judge."

"There was a most memorable author, whom I never had the opportunity to meet, but I did read much of his work. He once said, 'Never look back unless you are planning to go that way.' I like that quote."

I smile at the simplicity of the quote and question him. "Who was the author?"

Samuel answers, "Henry David Thoreau. I guess if one thinks about it, if I am sincere about what I do today, what difference does it make if I regret it tomorrow? Right?"

"Yes, Samuel. I see your point."

Samuel looks at me and motions me to follow him. We walk out the front door and over to his small vegetable garden.

The small plot appears to be well taken care of. The plantings are still very young, and I am unable to identify the seedlings. Fortunately, Samuel seems to be aware of my ignorance, and he begins to explain.

"As the Cherokee have always done, we plant only what we think we will eat. Since my family only consists of myself, my need is minimal. Thus, my garden is small. I have a couple rows of corn, there, a short row of tomatoes, two rows of beans, a row of cucumbers, and a row of squash. Of course, I supplement my diet with an occasional trip to the grocery store." He laughs at his own humor.

I watch Samuel as he stoops down and inspects the small seedlings. I say, "Samuel, I am amazed by your endurance at such age, but I don't understand why one, especially at your age, would plant and cultivate a garden, when it would be much more prudent to simply buy them all at the grocery."

"I find such pleasure in sinking my hands into the soil of the earth, planting the seeds, and feeling what the new season might bring. I think Abraham Lincoln said it best when he stated, 'The greatest fine art of the future will be the making of a comfortable living from a small piece of land.'"

Samuel and I walk down the street, and as we walk by each house, the neighbors come out onto their porches and wave at the two of us. They all recognize Samuel, of course, and greet him with such respect, I cannot help but take notice.

Samuel stops at each house and introduces me to each of his neighbors. He engages each neighbor in a sincere discussion of how things are with him or her. He questions by name of each member of the family, and on many occasions, the neighbor solicits him for advice. Samuel responds with such compassion and understanding that I begin to understand why he is held in such high regard.

We spend at least two hours walking just a few blocks because we spend much time with the neighbors. I find it very relaxing as well as uplifting to see Samuel interact with his people.

We walk slowly back to his house, and Samuel heats a pot of soup. We sit in the rockers on the front porch and eat our soup, chasing it with gulps of ice-cold buttermilk.

The sun dips low on the horizon, and Samuel suggests we start the drive back to Glen Choga before it becomes dark.

We drive the dark, snakelike road back to the lodge, to the glowing lights and the chatter of people.

When I get back to my room, I sit at my typewriter once again. The words are still not there; the typewriter seems to fight my efforts. I type, but the words appear on the page as meaningless gibberish. Instead I take a pen and paper and begin to write notes—short phrases, dates, and names to jog my memory when I am finally able to construct my literary masterpiece about Samuel.

I fall asleep staring at my dream catcher. Dreaming.

CHAPTER ELEVEN

War is what happens when language fails.

—Margaret Atwood

Once again, I wake later than usual. The sun's beacons of light sneak through the edges of the curtains, casting shimmering reflections on the walls of my room. I lie awake for thirty, maybe forty, minutes, thinking about Samuel and his story.

I hear other guests at the lodge moving about in the hallways outside my room, but I do not rise from my bed. I think about Samuel and imagine him sitting on the front porch in his rocker wondering where I am. I still lie motionless thinking.

I wonder if I will ever be able to hear the stars sing, to hear the star's melodies as Samuel. I begin to doubt myself. I think about Samuel and how he described his fear of being the didanawisgi. How he felt unprepared—or was it that he felt inferior to Gawonii, whom he replaced? I think about how Samuel had said he was not taught the answers but rather how to understand through compassion.

I feel I have learned so much the past few days, yet I'm unsure of what I have learned.

I rise from my bed and prepare to once again meet my friend Samuel.

I walk to the front porch, but Samuel is not there. I look out at the pond and the surrounding grounds, but there is no sight of Samuel. Alexander, the proprietor, speaks from the entrance of the lodge. "Jonathan, Samuel requested I tell you that if you were looking for him that you may find him on the back porch." Alexander smiled as if he knew something I did not.

I walk to the back porch and find Samuel sitting at the makeshift table where we had our dinner a few nights before. The cook, a negro, sits across from him, and they are laughing and playing a card game.

Samuel sees me and smiles warmly. He says, "Jonathan, come join us. We are playing a silly card game. Are you familiar with this game called War?"

I shake my head no and step closer to the table. The cook nods at me and stands. He smiles at Samuel and begins to move away but says, "Excuse me, sir. You may have my seat. I must get back to the kitchen." He hurries off toward the kitchen.

Samuel smiles and waves his hand at the empty seat. He says, "Franklin hates to lose. I've beaten him every game this morning. I was enjoying it myself, but apparently, he felt it too tiring. He lost the game, I lost his company; maybe I was right when I said that in war, there is never one who wins."

I sit opposite Samuel. He asks me, "Do you prefer War or some other silly game?"

I shrug and say, "I want you to teach me to hear the stars. I want you to teach me like Gawonii taught you—to find peace and wellness, balance with nature."

Samuel nods and says, "When one becomes hungry for food, the stomach is ready, and it is consumed with speed. When one is hungry for knowledge, the mind is ready as well, and then knowledge too is consumed with speed."

Samuel begins to tell his story.

"I maintained a close relationship with my good friend Booker T. Washington until he died around 1915. He and I continued to work together to ensure the funds were available to those that warranted them. In 1901, Booker T. was invited to dinner at the White House. Theodore Roosevelt was president then. I, being a business associate of Booker T., accompanied him.

"I found Roosevelt a very dynamic individual. During our dinner and meeting with Roosevelt, he questioned both Booker T. and I about the issue of civil rights. He listened intently as we both expressed our opinions and seemed to be intrigued with our observations on the topic.

"After the president listened, he leaned back in his chair, thought about what we had said, and then very bluntly began to share his thoughts on the subject. Basically, what he said was that he had not been able to think of any solution to the terrible problem the negroes present on this continent presented, but he did say that the only Christian thing to do was to judge a man, white or black, strictly on his merits as a man, and to give him the respect he was worthy of.

"After the president made his opinion known, Booker T. and I had differing opinions on how to react to his statement. Booker T. was somewhat discouraged and angered, but I understood it in a different way. I was somewhat encouraged to realize that the president recognized that the issue of equal rights was worthy of discussion.

"It was later in the evening when the president and I had stepped to an outside patio, he to smoke his cigar and I to smoke my pipe. He had been told that I was also Cherokee, and he began to question me about my experiences. It was quite a lively conversation. It may be considered by some to be a heated argument.

"I was disappointed to realize the president did not have a very good opinion of the Cherokee or, for that matter, any Indians. I think what he said was that he wouldn't go so far as to say the only good Indian is a dead one—maybe nine out of ten are better dead, and that's without looking too deep into the character of the tenth one.

"I began to rethink my opinion of Teddy Roosevelt.

"Right around 1900, I met Gifford Pinchot. He was the first man I had ever met that had dedicated his life to forestry and land conservation. There had been several people, including myself, that had a great amount of respect for the land and forests, and we each had strong opinions on the subject. Pinchot took it a step further. He turned the idea of land conservation and forestry into a science.

"I met him first when he was commissioned by George Vanderbilt of the Biltmore Estate to manage the forest lands surrounding the estate. Pinchot was an extreme conservationist. During this time in history, there were only a few that spoke outwardly about the necessity to either preserve or conserve our natural resources and our forests. It was a relatively new concept, and there were differing opinions on whether to simply preserve or to conserve. Pinchot was a conservationist."

Samuel stands and motions me to follow him. I am anxious to hear more of his story, but I'm not in the mood for another long walk. I ask him, "Samuel, you're not taking me on another long walk, are you?"

Samuel chuckles and shakes his head no. He says, "No, Jonathan. But there is something I would like you to see. It's only a short walk."

I stand and follow him into the woods and up the hillside behind the lodge. We walk maybe half a mile to the top of a ridgeline, and Samuel motions me to have a seat next to him on a rock outcropping overlooking the valley to the southeast.

I sit and stare across the expanse before me. The rolling mountains appear to go on forever. The deep-green foliage of the forests covers the steep slopes, rising upward till it disappears into the white, puffy clouds above.

Samuel continues. “Pinchot was a brilliant man when it came to forestry, but he was an extreme conservationist, which did not sit well with other leaders in the forestry field. Carl Schenck and John Muir both were naturalists and were very intelligent, but they were more preservationists, and there was always conflict between the groups as to what was best. I like to think the Cherokee had always practiced conservation but never knew the term. The Cherokee had a great respect for nature, its forests, and its streams and only took from it what was necessary.

“When Pinchot was brought to the Biltmore Estate, he took it upon himself to gather as many people as he could that shared his opinions on conservationism. I was one he called upon. I was impressed with his knowledge as well as his dedication to his ideals, and I think he found the Cherokee way very ingenious. We became very good friends, but he was eventually replaced with one of the many that believed in preservation of the forests rather than conservation.

“After he left Biltmore, Pinchot was named chief of the US Forest Service by President Theodore Roosevelt in 1905. Pinchot and I had remained friends for all those years, and on several occasions, I was invited by my good friend Pinchot to attend functions in Washington, DC, but I always declined. I feared, based on Roosevelt’s opinion of the Indians, that if I showed, I might have been shot by the president himself.”

Samuel laughed out loud, and I did as well. It was a statement meant to be funny, yet it rang with a bit of truth.

I could almost imagine the fiery Theodore Roosevelt, dressed in his Rough Rider attire, standing in front of old, quiet Samuel. Samuel in all his wisdom listens to the president’s abusive remarks without argument. Then when the president is through, Samuel stands, pounds his chest and says, "Look deep, look here. Now what do you see?"

The image makes me laugh to myself.

Samuel continues. "Woodrow Wilson was elected president, and like now, a war in Europe seemed imminent. I was impressed with the president's resolve for the United States to remain neutral in the conflict. He was content to involve us only with diplomacy and of course—maybe a mistake on his part—finances and supplies to our allies.

"There was a tremendous amount of pressure from others in the political arena to send troops or at least to involve the navy in the conflict. Wilson persevered until the sinking of the *Lusitania*, where a hundred or more American lives were lost. My friend Theodore Roosevelt led a campaign to pressure Wilson to enter the war, stopping the piratical tactics of the Germans and their submarines.

"President Wilson was receiving a lot of pressure from a lot of politicians, as well as many of the people of the nation, to enter the war. He, like some would say, was between a rock and a hard place. Wilson began to put together a team of individuals, prominent peace leaders that could stand independent of the constraints of Congress, to help broker a peace in Europe. Some might claim that it was a little like a covert operation put together by Wilson. In his opinion, as well as of those that participated, he just made it possible for a group of people with the same goals of peace be brought together. From that point on, the president was not involved.

"I felt honored when I was summoned by President Wilson to Washington in these regards.

"Once there, I realized there were several hundred leaders from all walks of life. Everyone had been summoned and brought together to help broker a peace but was independent of any government involvement or government finances.

"One of the participants I became very close with—for we shared similar opinions on the matter—was Henry Ford. He felt war in general was a terrible waste, and he became highly critical of those who he felt helped finance the conflict in Europe. I and many others felt the same.

"In 1915, the group of a little over one hundred people traveled to Sweden to meet with other peace activists to develop a plan to broker a peace. I was one of those that accompanied them.

"President Wilson was aware of our mission, but we did not receive any government support. It was funded solely by Ford, myself, and a few others.

"I had great hopes of what we might accomplish, and even though I was much older than anyone else involved, and much less prominent of a leader, I was consulted by many of the group regarding my ideas. The issues we discussed were quite complex. Many of the participants had a tremendous amount of knowledge on the issues and at times could be intimidating.

"I remember listening to the group and feeling so incompetent. The discussion had become very heated. Everyone seemed to have a different opinion, and many began to shout at others. I sat there feeling too impotent to discuss such complex problems, but then, somewhere within, I heard Gawonii speaking to me. His soft-spoken voice, his compassion, and all his wisdom seemed to fill me. I stood, and it seemed to take all the participants by surprise, for I had never been so bold as to engage myself in such a heated debate. I began to recite the words I heard from Gawonii.

"The large group sat silently listening to my reasoning. No one spoke in opposition to the reasoning I presented. I was not sure if they were just being respectful because of my age, or maybe it was because I was colored, but they listened, intrigued, and when I finished, they all stood and gave me a standing ovation.

"That was one of the first times of my life that I began to feel confident in being didanawisgi, a Cherokee medicine man. I began to realize the power does not come from myself, but from the soul given to me by Gawonii. I began to feel even freer and more liberated than before.

"Unfortunately, our group of peacemakers was not successful in our efforts to broker a peace, but I believe all the ones that participated in the effort became a little more understanding and compassionate of others. They began to realize that only through understanding is lasting peace ever achieved."

I listen to Samuel as he relates his story, and I have a very vivid image of the old man standing before the large crowd of peacemakers and making his point. I can imagine the crowd sitting silent and moved by Samuel's reasoning and resolve, much like I have been.

I say to Samuel, "I admire your efforts to broker a peace, but you were not successful. There was a war. So maybe there are times that peace cannot be achieved."

Samuel smiles and says, "There were many that were convinced that peace was possible, but it would only be achieved when more of mankind could understand. Even though there was a war, I was at peace within myself. It would have been nice if there had been many more that felt the peace within as I."

I say in response, "So in your opinion, there is never a just cause for war?"

"I will not say never, but I can't fathom something so egregious to warrant a war. It's been said that if the power of love overcomes the love of power, then the world will find peace."

I look at Samuel. "And the Confederates that were raping and killing your people? Did they not warrant what you did that day?"

Samuel looks terribly saddened but shakes his head no. He says, "I have lived with the sorrow for my actions that day my whole life. If I had been wiser, more compassionate, and more understanding, I may have prevented it from happening. That is my belief. I am only a man. I have made mistakes."

I say, "I don't think any man would have reacted any different than you in that circumstance. You should not feel any guilt."

"Please try to explain that to the widowed wives, the fatherless children, the brothers and sisters, the mothers and fathers of those men I killed. They may have a differing opinion."

Samuel stands and stretches. He gazes across the valley below, and then studies the sky above. White, puffy clouds litter the deep-blue sky, and he smiles. A slight breeze ruffles his long white hair as he turns his face upward seeking the warmth of the sun, the view of the heavens above, and possibly seeking the forgiveness of God as well.

CHAPTER TWELVE

No man is above the law, and no man is below it.

—Theodore Roosevelt

Samuel and I walk the short distance back to the lodge and have our lunch on the front lawn next to the pond.

We talk leisurely over our lunch. Samuel is curious as to my history. He questions me about where I am from and what my family life was like and asks details about my education. He seems most interested, and I find that strange. How can he find any interest in my mundane story when he has lived such an eventful and adventurous life?

He asks, "And your job with the paper. Do you find it rewarding?"

I think about the question for a moment and then give him the best answer I have. "I have not been out of school long and have only worked there for a little over two years. I have felt, in the past, that I have not been given the opportunity to show my real talent, but now I'm beginning to realize that I may not have had the talent

I thought I had. I have come to realize that maybe I was not as sensitive to the *real* story as I should have been, and now that I have found a story that is inspiring, I cannot find the words to express it adequately. I'm beginning to feel somewhat like a failure."

Samuel pats me on the shoulder as if to give me a little encouragement and says, "Thoreau once said, 'Be yourself, not your idea of what you think somebody else's idea of yourself should be.'" Samuel then continues, explaining his thoughts. "Feeling the inspiration is a gift in itself. Treasure that ability, for there are some incapable of feeling emotion. Words are nothing more than a way to paint those emotions you feel. Let your heart choose the words and not your grammatically correct, literary senses. I think the words your heart chooses will be much more representative of your emotions."

I nod in agreement, realizing that Samuel has just given me an invaluable lesson in journalism. I say, "I understand what you are saying, and I agree, but the words are just not there."

Samuel grins and says, "When you first saw me, that first morning, what words would you have chosen to describe me?"

I say, "Aged, black man; long white hair and white beard; soft-spoken."

Samuel says, "And what words would you choose to describe me now?"

I smile, for I know what he is doing. "Wise, intriguing, spiritual, compassionate."

"You see, Jonathan, you are now letting your emotions and your heart choose the words. You are very capable. I am glad you have been chosen to write my story."

Samuel tells me more of his story.

"With all the good intentions of President Wilson to try to broker a peace concerning the war in Europe, I was disappointed in his ability to promote equal rights for the colored. I was fortunate to have met him on several occasions, and as hostile as Roosevelt was to me for being Cherokee, Wilson was as hostile to me for being colored. Both Roosevelt and Wilson seemed to accept me personally, but they had a dislike for the races I represented. During his presidency, Wilson undid much of our civil- and equal-rights accomplishments. During Roosevelt's term, most of the government became integrated, and the murderous lynchings of the South had slowed, but with Wilson, it reversed.

"Wilson was a Southern Democrat, and one of those had not been elected to the presidency since the 1840s. To the Southerners, it was a major victory, and they hoped to see a rebirth of the old, racist policies of the early Southern leaders.

"Monroe Trotter, who was an editor for the Boston newspaper and an acquaintance, brought together a few of us to travel to the White House to protest President Wilson's segregation policies. The president remembered me from my efforts to bring peace before the First World War and treated me kindly, but he treated our group rudely, telling us that segregation is not a humiliation but a benefit, and we should regard it as such. We all went back to our homes feeling as if we had failed terribly.

"It was upsetting to us to have worked so hard and invested so much of our time and money in trying to acquire equal rights for all, just to have them ignored once again.

"You might find it interesting that my friend Monroe Trotter, the editor of the Boston newspaper, was also a Harvard graduate.

"It was during Taft's first term that my good friend W. E. B. Du Bois, an early beneficiary of my funding, formed an organization dedicated to secure equal rights for all individuals as stated in the Thirteenth, Fourteenth, and Fifteenth Amendments of the Constitution. The organization was called the National Association for the Advancement of Colored People; most just called it the NAACP.

"This organization brought together a large group of various individuals who had been promoting equal rights in their own individual way. Unified within this organization, they became much more effective in their efforts. It brought me a great sense of satisfaction to see so many individuals, white and black, come together with the same goals in mind. I felt my efforts in funding many of these individuals over the past forty years had helped this come to fruition.

"In the beginning, the organization sought first to make whites aware of the need for racial equality. They accomplished this through speechmaking, lobbying, and publicizing the issue. Friends of mine such as Booker T. Washington, W. E. B. Du Bois, and many others used their oratory and literary talents in this effort. I was very proud of them.

"Later, the organization used their power and their growing wealth to challenge segregation and racial inequality in the courts. The organization became a worthy power for the segregationists and opponents to equal rights to deal with.

"Keep in mind that by this time, I was in my midseventies, and my influence with the NAACP was negligible. I maintained a very close friendship with Booker T. as well as Du Bois, but I participated very little with any of the policy making of the organization. It seemed as if my major contribution to the organization was that I was a common friend or acquaintance to most of these individuals who came together to help form and promote the NAACP.

"There were many occasions when I would visit Booker T. and eat dinner with him and his family. I remember having many interesting conversations with Margaret, Booker T.'s wife. Her opinions on civil rights were much like my own, and I think we both found some satisfaction to find someone who had similar ideas.

"Booker T. and Du Bois had very different ideas on how to promote equality for the blacks, and this began to divide their friendship, which I worked hard at trying to retain for them both.

"They both were extremely intelligent and articulate, but Du Bois wanted to address issues head on. He could be accusatory and inflaming to the whites that opposed his beliefs. Booker T. wanted the same as Du Bois, but he felt more could be accomplished if you found some common ground with the whites and work through compromise.

"Both of their methods had worked for each one, but their differences would eventually ruin their friendship. I was fortunate to consider each a dear friend and kept my friendship with Booker T. till he died about fifteen years ago, and I still maintain a close friendship with Du Bois."

I find these relationships of Samuel interesting, and I question him. "Samuel, were any of these friends of yours aware of the gold? Where the money was coming from?"

Samuel chuckles quietly and says, "If I was someone seeking a loan, there would have been many questions—questions about why I needed the loan, my ability to repay, and my net worth. If you are giving money, regardless of the amount, the beneficiaries are not concerned with its origin. They never questioned me about it."

"I am curious, Samuel. If they had questioned you, would you have told them?"

"Yes, of course. I loved these people as brothers, and there was a tremendous amount of trust between us. I think that is why they never questioned me. They trusted and loved me as well."

I am still a little confused about how such a large amount of gold had been dispersed to so many without any question—or, for that matter, any government inquisitions. I continue questioning him. "When you approached your friend Booker T. to set up the trusts, how did the gold get transferred? Surely you did not personally load the gold and carry it to the banks."

Samuel laughs out loud at my remark, and I feel embarrassed. He says, "Given my age when most the gold was removed from the cave, I could not have lifted a single bar without the aid of a friend."

Samuel continues, "Booker T. and I enlisted the aid of a group of close to fifty men. These men were close friends and people we trusted. We acquired the necessary equipment and vehicles and divided the gold in manageable quantities. We called these manageable quantities 'blocks,' and they amounted to ten bars to each block. These blocks, of which there were forty-nine, were distributed to a variety of banks and financial institutions. This was done under a variety of individual names, institutions, and corporations. A little over half was deposited in financial institutions outside of the United States. It was a very elaborate process to accomplish, but it had to be done. I would have never been able to move all of that gold by myself."

"And no one ever questioned you about where all of the gold had come from?"

"No."

I shake my head in disbelief. "And how much do you imagine is still left?"

Samuel grins and says, "Forty-eight blocks, I think. There is still an unimaginable amount left."

"So we are talking about millions of dollars' worth?"

"Hundreds of millions." Samuel looks at me very seriously and says, "Most of the funds I used to finance the equal-rights movement in the beginning actually went to individuals whom I trusted. They eventually became very successful. With their success, they began to invest in the movement themselves, so eventually, very little of the gold was used over time.

"The funds were not only used for the advancement of colored people but were also used to help Native Americans, the Indians. Strict guidelines were placed as to how these funds were to be spent. I, and others, did not want to simply buy or pay their way into society. We purposely wanted to merely support their endeavors to advance their quality of life. We did so by financing bonds to aid in building or rebuilding much of the infrastructures of their communities. It gave them an opportunity to succeed, which they would not have had otherwise."

Thomas, my photographer, walks from the lodge toward Samuel and me. He is carrying his camera and appears to be in a hurry. He arrives out of breath and red faced. He says, "Jonathan, please forgive my interruption, but I just received a phone call from Harold Sims." He glances at me with a worried look. "Jonathan, he seemed somewhat upset. I think he may have expected you back in New York by now. He said he had wanted you to be at the World's Fair opening ceremonies."

I feel a pain of concern in my gut, and Thomas continues, "Jonathan, he was pretty angry. He told me to find you and have you call him immediately."

The pain of concern that had overtaken me just a few seconds before gave way to a wave of anger. The anger began to consume me in its entirety. I start to voice my opinion to Thomas and Samuel; instead, I keep the thoughts to myself. I wonder how in the world Sims could be the least bit upset. I had talked with him just two days before, and he couldn't even remember who I was or the assignment I was on. He had never mentioned to me at any time wanting me there for the World's Fair. I am as angry as I think I have ever been.

I stand and tell the two before me, "Well, I guess I should call my boss." I grin, but it's a superficial grin, for I am still furious within.

Samuel grabs my arm as I began to walk back to the lodge, and he smiles kindly and says, "Please remember, Jonathan, that lasting peace can only be achieved through understanding and compassion."

I walk toward the lodge to use the phone, and I think about what Samuel has just said.

I dial Sims's number, and to my surprise, Sims answers on the first ring. "Hello, Sims here."

He sounds angry. I say, "Hello, Harold, Jonathan Newcastle here. I understand you requested I call you."

"Jonathan, the World's Fair opening ceremonies begin today. I need you here to help cover it. What in the hell could you be doing down there in the boonies that is so interesting to keep you for five days?"

"I am so sorry, Harold. I assumed you wanted me to get all the details of one of the most intriguing and magnificent stories of all time. I am flattered that you would have even considered someone like me, who has very little journalistic experience, cover such a story as that of Samuel Timmons. I also understand the importance of the beginning of the World's Fair there in New York and am likewise flattered that you would consider me to attend on the behalf of the *Times*. If you think I would be of better service there in New York, I will have Thomas drive me at once to the train station. I could most likely be there by morning."

Sims is quiet on the other end. I can hear his brain working, thinking. He finally speaks in a much friendlier tone and asks, "And what makes this Samuel Timmons so interesting?"

"Samuel has lived over a hundred years. That is most intriguing, but to understand the years he had spent as a slave, the heroic escape to freedom, the most emotional life he spent as a Cherokee—and all of this interlaced with elements of rape, murder, war, staggering amounts of wealth, and ties with at least three different presidents of the United States—I think most anyone would find it to be of interest. I am sorry if I assumed wrong in your desire for me to cover this story in detail. I did not realize how interesting and complex this story was, but I'm sure you were aware of this story's potential, and I am honored you considered me to be here."

Sims is quiet once again, and I wait expectantly. He finally says, "Yes…of course, Jonathan. I figured Samuel Timmons would have an interesting story. I just want to make sure you are progressing nicely with a story such as this. I do realize you are relatively inexperienced and just want you to understand that I am here to help you."

"Thank you, Harold. I appreciate having someone like you with all of your experience to be there as my mentor."

"Very well then, Jonathan. I have others here to help cover the World's Fair. Please keep me posted as to your progress with the story of Samuel. Thank you for returning my call." And Sims hangs up.

I breathe a sigh of relief. I realize I am sweating profusely with nerves. I stand holding the phone's receiver and shaking. I think to myself, "Peace through understanding and compassion." I had been ready to tell Sims exactly my thoughts. I was prepared to tell him to take the job and shove it, but Samuel had set me right. The words I chose with Sims seemed not to be mine. They had come from I know not where, for I would not have thought to speak so rationally in the situation that had been given me. Were they words given to me subconsciously by Samuel? Or were they words from Gawonii?

I walk somewhat proudly back to the pond where Thomas was snapping pictures of the relaxing Samuel. As I approach, both Samuel and Thomas look at me questioningly. I say, "Harold was most understanding. He suggested I stay and complete this assignment."

Thomas looked as if he didn't believe me, and Samuel just smiled.

I sit beside Samuel once again, and Thomas continues taking pictures of the two of us. Both Samuel and I just ignore the busy photographer as he circles the two of us snapping his pictures. I look at Samuel and say, "I think I heard the voices you have spoken of so frequently. The words came to me with such ease I found it very easy to convince my boss I should stay here and complete this story."

Samuel nods and smiles. He says, "You are now feeding the good wolf in your soul. Now, let me tell you some more of my story.

"After World War I, there was a period of relative prosperity in the United States. Part of this was a result of the industrialization of the United States that occurred just prior to the war, and the other part was the repayment of the loans the United States had given to their allies, such as Great Britain and France. We survived the devastation of the war in better shape than before the war, although all that prosperity was not to last, as you well know.

"In 1920, I was introduced to a rather famous attorney in Cincinnati, Ohio. His name was George Remus. At the time of the first meeting, it seemed to have happened by circumstance. I was involved in a convention of the NAACP in Cincinnati, and a lawyer that represented the organization insisted I meet one of his constituents. It was George Remus.

"I discovered a short time into the introduction that Remus was a criminal defense attorney and had acquired notoriety in defending some of the most unscrupulous people.

"I listened as Remus described a plan he had devised. It was a plan to utilize loopholes within the Eighteenth Amendment and the Volstead Act that enabled him to manufacture and distribute alcohol legally. As you know, 1920 was the year Prohibition began.

"Remus's plan was ingenious, but in my opinion, it was terribly immoral.

"I declined his offer to participate in his undertaking. He wanted me to use my influence within the colored community as well as my Cherokee influences to distribute large quantities of his legal distillates. I realized even then that although he was manufacturing the alcohol legally, the distribution of such, as he suggested, was of a criminal nature.

"I think he thought that I, being about eighty years old, would be gullible as well as greedy and would accept his offer without much thought. He was terribly angry when I smiled at him and said, 'No, thank you.'

"What I found odd was that at that time, I did not feel I had that much influence within the colored community nor with the Cherokee, but by him seeking my support with such determination, I began to realize…I did.

"Remus was terribly unscrupulous, and I feared that after I declined his offer, he would circumvent me and seek the distribution channels he desired through others within the colored and Cherokee communities. I began an intensive campaign against Remus using my influence in those same communities.

"Remus was furious and set about to get rid of my interference in his plan. At first, they were just idle threats; then came legal suits, not to myself, but to organizations I was a part of, and then came actual threats to my life. I cannot say I was unaffected by his efforts, because I was, but I did not yield.

"In 1925, he was convicted on several violations of the Volstead Act and spent two years in federal prison. By the time he got out, everyone who had been connected to him had taken most everything he had owned. He was ruined."

I listened to Samuel tell his story, and I felt a sense of extreme admiration. I don't think I had ever felt such high respect for anyone before as I did for Samuel. I found Samuel extremely wise and compassionate and his morals to be that of a saint. I say, "I remember learning about George Remus in my classes at Harvard. I had learned Remus was very corrupt but also probably the wealthiest man in the United States. Knowing what I know, I am amazed you did not become a part of his plan."

"In my life, I have lost many people dear to me for the sake of freedom. There is no amount of money that could be offered me to relinquish the freedom I've acquired. If I had accepted Remus's offer, I would have become enslaved once again—owned and shackled by his wealth and power. I found it easier to escape him than I did my previous master, Ethan Jackson."

Thomas finishes taking his photos and informs us he is going to take a nap. I nod his way and say, "Yes, you've had an eventful day, Thomas. Why don't you take off the rest of the afternoon?"

Thomas walks slowly back toward the lodge, and the sun begins to lie low on the horizon.

Samuel and I sit in silence as we each savor the ambience of the front lawn. The pond, the sounds of the forest that surrounds us, the ducks with their occasional quacks, the almost continuous hum of bees that fly about, and the chirping of sparrows seem to encourage the silence.

A car drives up the long drive, sending clouds of dust into the air. Samuel and I glance at the automobile as it comes to a halt in front of the lodge.

A few moments later, a young negro who is dressed very fashionably, approaches us. He seems timid to approach but does so anyway. He says, "Mr. Timmons, I am here on behalf of Mr. McKinney from Atlanta. He has sent me to request you join me and return immediately to Atlanta. He has some issues of most importance to discuss with you."

Samuel stands unsteadily at first but soon regains his balance. He shakes the young man's hand and says, "What is your name, young man?"

"Charles Houston sir."

Samuel smiles broadly and says, "Yes, I have heard of you. It is so nice to finally meet you. May I introduce my friend, Jonathan Newcastle? He is a famous reporter for the *New York Times*. Somehow, they find what I have to say of some importance." Samuel laughs.

Charles nods and says, "Everyone thinks what you have to say is important. May I convince you to join me in Atlanta?"

Samuel seems to think a moment and then says, "May my friend Jonathan join us? We still have a lot to discuss, and his time—well, it is much more important than mine."

"Most certainly, Mr. Timmons. I will notify Mr. McKinney and arrange rooms for you both at the Ellis Hotel."

Samuel glances at me and smiles.

I say, "I must pack my belongings. When should we plan to depart?"

Charles nods and responds, "As soon as the two of you are ready, sir."

CHAPTER THIRTEEN

Too often we underestimate the power of a touch, a smile, a kind word, a listening ear, an honest compliment, or the smallest act of caring, all of which have the potential to turn a life around.

—Leo Buscaglia

Within an hour, both Samuel and I are in the Ford coupe. Charles drives the three of us toward Atlanta. It will be a three- to four-hour drive, but I am excited beyond belief.

Only one thing concerns me: the fact that my clothes look as if I had slept in them for the past six days. My shoes are scuffed and covered in mud. My hair and general appearance look as though I have had performed no personal hygiene. I question Samuel with concern. "Excuse me, Samuel. I only brought this set of clothes with me from New York, and as you can see, they are not very appropriate for your friends in Atlanta."

Samuel grins and says, "We will have Charles stop at Thompson's in Atlanta. You can purchase what you need there."

I look at Samuel and say, "Unfortunately, Samuel, I cannot afford to buy a whole new wardrobe. Maybe I can just have this laundered."

Samuel says, "Tell them you work for the *New York Times*, and give them Harold Sims's name. I'm sure they will get paid; plus, they will feel they have been a part of greatness." He nods at me sincerely. I agree.

For the first hour, maybe two, we travel through similar terrain. Mountains, woods, and very few dwellings. Then the landscape begins to level. There are rolling hills, more pastures, more homes, and more people. We stop to get gasoline, and we each buy a Coca-Cola. Samuel buys peanuts and pours them into the tapered bottle of cola.

The sun sets, and our surroundings disappear in the darkness. We travel within our cocoon of metal and the thrumming engine. I feel it an adventure I could only dream.

In the darkest of night, we arrive at the Ellis Hotel in downtown Atlanta. It is late, maybe ten at night. The streets are almost void of activity. The bellboys scurry to gather our bags and usher us into the hotel's lobby.

It is most magnificent. It is not nearly as flamboyant as the Waldorf in New York, but is very elegant all the same. There is a charm about the place, I should say. I am immediately reminded of my appearance, but everyone seems not to notice, for they are focused on my friend Samuel. They know him by name and bow to him as if he is royalty. I follow as if I'm invisible.

Charles gives a friendly hug to Samuel and says he will return early to carry us where we need to be.

Samuel says, "First things first. My friend Jonathan requests some new attire. He has traveled far and endured much; we must make sure he acquires the necessary attentions to be presentable."

"Yes, of course. I will take you and Mr. Newcastle to Thompson's first thing in the morning. It has been an honor to meet you, Mr.

Timmons." Charles then looks at me as if forgetting. "And you, as well Mr. Newcastle."

"Yes. Thank you for your attention," I say.

Charles leaves, and Samuel and I sit in the lobby of the Ellis alone. It's a large hotel and very elaborate, but it is late. The guests have had their fun and are now in their rooms, leaving Samuel and I alone to wonder what is to come of tomorrow.

Samuel asks, "Are you familiar with William McKinney?"

I think and say, "No, I do not think I know the name."

Samuel answers, "He is one of the founders of the NAACP. An attorney, a unique individual, and a very dear friend. I should add that he too is a journalist. I look forward to you meeting him."

The name McKinney is familiar, but I can't understand why. I say, "I look forward to meeting him as well."

Samuel and I agree that it is time we retire for the evening.

The next morning, I awake with a sense of anxiety. It may have been the long drive, the surreal events from the previous day, or simply my fatigue, but when I wake, I am terribly excited for what is to come.

Charles arrives and takes me to Thompson's, a fine clothier in Atlanta. I am somewhat embarrassed by my appearance, but both Samuel and Charles take charge, and soon I am dressed immaculately.

I tell the clothier to bill the *New York Times*, and Harold Sims, for the expense, and I walk out with a new wardrobe.

I don't know if it is the clothes or simply the experience, but I feel empowered. I feel important.

Samuel looks me up and down and nods his approval. He himself has transformed. He is dressed in a very fashionable tweed suit. His long white hair billows beyond the collars, and his beard appears to interfere with the ensemble, but he looks very distinguished. He smiles and nods his approval as I approach.

I say, "You look debonair, Samuel. Shall we go meet your friend?"

"You look very nice yourself, Jonathan. Yes, we must go and meet with McKinney."

Charles drives us downtown to a nondescript office building where McKinney's office is located and much of the NAACP planning and administration takes place. The three of us enter, and I am surprised to find that the offices abound with activity. There are thirty, maybe forty, staff running here and running there. Some are on phones, and some shuffle papers; all seem to be in a panic.

Charles takes us directly to McKinney's office. McKinney, a very distinguished-looking white man, stands and smiles broadly as Samuel enters. McKinney and Samuel hug each other as good friends do and then shake hands. I can tell there is a tremendous amount of respect shared between them.

Samuel says, "Oh, please forgive me. William, I would like for you to meet my good friend and a very successful journalist for the *New York Times.* This is Jonathan Newcastle. Jonathan, this is my good friend and very important member of the NAACP, William McKinney. Not only is William one of the founders of NAACP, but he is a journalist as well, and I should add, a very successful attorney who has helped our organization immensely."

We shake hands, and McKinney gestures for us to have a seat. He pulls his desk chair from behind his desk, and we three sit in a semicircle.

McKinney is tall and has a very distinguished look. He has white hair, which is styled very fashionably, and he looks to be in his midsixties. My first impression of him is that he is kind and genuine but is mostly about the business at hand.

McKinney says, "Samuel, please forgive me for dragging you to Atlanta on such short notice, but we have an issue that I think warrants your input as well as possibly your influence."

Samuel smiles and nods. He replies, "William, I am always more than happy to help with our cause. What issue has arisen that is of such concern?"

McKinney sits back in his chair and carefully chooses his words. He says, "Samuel, as you are aware, the highly acclaimed movie *Gone with the Wind* is scheduled to have its premiere here in Atlanta in December. It will attract an enormous amount of publicity. What has been brought to our attention and is of tremendous concern is that they are not allowing any of the black stars of the movie to attend. They are not even allowing the photographs of the colored in the souvenir program of the gala. Neither Hattie McDaniel nor Butterfly McQueen is being allowed to participate in the event. I find this terribly racist, and the colored community does as well. I'm afraid of the repercussions this may have within the colored community of Atlanta and elsewhere. We have submitted letters of disapproval to the ones in charge, but they have refused to change their mind. We, the NAACP, had hoped that maybe you could use your influence and convince those involved to reconsider."

Samuel stands from his chair and walks to a window that looks out to the busy street outside. He stares at nothing but says, "And have you spoken to Hattie and Butterfly? Are they upset about not being included in the premiere here in Atlanta?"

McKinney shrugs and says, "No. We have not spoken with either of them, but surely they are displeased not to be included."

Samuel replies, "Please have someone contact them immediately. I would very much like to hear their opinion."

McKinney says, "Yes, I will have my assistant contact them. Samuel, this is blatant discrimination. I'm afraid that if we allow this to happen, we might have another riot like the one in 1906."

Samuel turns from the window and says, "William, what if Hattie and Butterfly would rather we not pursue their inclusion? What if they are afraid of the animosity that such a demand might cause between them and their employers? It is not as simple as *making* the whites do what is just. We must encourage the whites to *want* to do what is just. We must be very careful in situations as this. If done improperly, even if we succeed in getting what we want, it can create an even further separation between the whites and the colored. "

William sits quietly thinking. He is tapping a pencil on the desk beside him as he thinks. He says, "Yes, Samuel, I see your point. Unfortunately, there is a scheduled meeting I have with David Selznick, the producer of the film, Mayor Hartsfield, and Governor Rivers this afternoon and would like very much you attend. We must at least voice our displeasure."

Samuel smiles and says, "Jonathan and I would very much like to attend this meeting. I know the mayor well but have not had the opportunity to meet the governor or Selznick. I would very much like to listen to their opinion on this matter."

I am aghast at the calmness Samuel possesses. Even McKinney seems to be in a tizzy with the events, and now that Samuel has invited me along, I too feel in a panic. Never would I have thought I would be in a meeting with David Selznick, the mayor of Atlanta, and the governor of Georgia discussing a movie that is being touted as the greatest movie of all time.

McKinney stands and walks over to shake Samuel's hand once again. He says, "Thank you, Samuel. I was hoping I could count on you. I will have Charles take you and Jonathan to the governor's mansion. The meeting is at two o'clock."

Samuel says, "Very well then. Please contact me when your assistant locates Hattie and Butterfly. I would very much like to discuss this with them both before our meeting; after all, it's more about them than anything else."

As Samuel and I are preparing to leave, I notice McKinney's desk. It is covered with paper, notes, newspaper clippings, and legal documents. There are also photographs standing in frames and proudly displayed. I see McKinney with the president and other dignitaries I cannot identify. I see a family photograph;

apparently, he and his wife have three children. And I see another photograph of a lady I know. It is Allison—Allison McKinney.

I say, "Excuse me, Mr. McKinney. May I ask—is Allison your granddaughter?"

McKinney smiles broadly and says, "Yes. She surely is. Do you know Allison?"

"Yes. We have met. I found her to be quite interesting. I do not know her well; we only met on the train when I came to North Carolina. She did mention you."

McKinney smiles again and says, "I will tell her I met her friend Jonathan. She will most assuredly be pleased to hear you are in town."

Samuel and I leave the office, and Charles takes Samuel and me back to our hotel.

The Ellis hotel is very elaborate, even by New York standards. The lobby is large with marble floors and grand chandeliers hanging throughout. Bellboys scurry about tending to the guests' needs. Samuel and I find a sitting area not far from the concierge and relax in two oversized chairs.

Samuel takes out his corncob pipe and begins to smoke. He says, "Well, Jonathan, at least you will have something interesting to write about." He chuckles.

"Yes, Samuel, that I will."

One of the bellboys approaches and says, "Excuse me, Mr. Timmons? There is a phone call at the front desk for you."

Samuel gets up and walks to the front desk. He is on the phone for about ten minutes, and then he returns to where I am sitting. He says, "Well, that was Hattie McDaniel, one of the black actresses in the movie we were discussing earlier this morning. Just what I expected. She is very much aware of her and the other black cast members being excluded in the premiere here in Atlanta. As expected, she would rather not make much of it because of the possibility of repercussions within the industry she works in."

I look at Samuel, and he does not appear to be concerned in any way. I ask, "So what do we do now? Do we still go to the meeting?"

Samuel smiles and says, "Of course. I've never met the governor and very much want to do so. I also want to make sure they take ownership in choosing to be this discriminatory. I know they will cite the Jim Crow laws as the reason. I just want them to say it. When this movie is everything they say it is going to be, and Hattie McDaniel and the others are recognized for their performances, these men we are to meet will have some explaining to do for excluding them. It is a way to make them understand the value of integration without forcing them and creating animosity."

"Makes sense, Samuel. But do you not feel as if you are in some ways giving in to them?"

"Not at all, Jonathan. I'll have questions for them. They will answer, and they must own it at that time. They will feel proud of themselves that they won, but they will not feel proud for long. I believe they will regret not including all of the cast, especially if Hattie and Butterfly win Oscars for their performances."

Samuel and I go to the hotel's dining room to have our lunch, and once again Samuel informs me he will not be allowed to eat in the main dining room. Coloreds cannot eat with the whites. I say, "That is so crazy, Samuel. You are not like the rest. Why can you not eat with me?"

Samuel looks at me and says, "I am colored just like the rest. That seems to be what matters. Most have not learned to look deep, in here, as you have, Jonathan." And he pounds his chest and smiles. He continues. "Go eat your lunch where you are accustomed, and I will have mine where I feel comfortable. Charles will be by shortly to carry us to the governor's house." He turns and walks to a side door that has a sign posted: Coloreds' Dining.

I walk into the main dining room alone.

I sit at my table alone. I order from a colored waiter, and I finally understand Samuel!

I begin to write. I write on my napkin and on pieces of paper I have stuffed in my pockets. I jot down notes, tidbits of information, things to jog my memory. I now understand.

I am free!

CHAPTER FOURTEEN

One thing you learn when you've lived as long as I have—people aren't all good, and people aren't all bad. We move in and out of darkness and light all of our lives. Right now, I'm pleased to be in the light.

—Neal Shusterman

My lunch is great. It would have been better if I had someone to share a conversation with. I imagine Samuel enjoying conversation with the kitchen staff—he sharing his tidbits of wisdom and they bowing as if he were royalty. I wish I were there, not necessarily to watch the staff stand in reverence but to share those moments of enlightenment.

I finish my lunch and sit watching the other people. Couples smiling, flirting, playing their games. I see businesspeople, stern and angry, trying to come to agreement. I see the ones that are mute, unable to voice their opinions and thoughts, and I try to read their minds. Then I see Samuel. He is standing at the door, waving to me. He is saying, "It's time to go."

I tell the waiter to bill my lunch to Harold Sims at the *New York Times.*

Charles is waiting for us at the front entrance.

William McKinney is in the front seat of the automobile as Samuel and I climb into the back. Charles drives our group the short ten miles to the governor's mansion.

Samuel and Charles chat the whole way there while McKinney and I sit silent, our nerves in a bundle in anticipation of the meeting.

The governor's mansion is a beautiful place, and I notice there are several security officers strolling about the grounds. They stop our car as we pull into the driveway.

Charles explains to the officer our purpose, and he waves us through.

We are taken into the mansion by another security officer and guided into a large sitting room. There is no one else there.

In just a few minutes, Governor Rivers enters the room. He smiles and approaches William McKinney first. They shake hands and exchange pleasantries, and McKinney begins to introduce us to the governor.

As the introductions are being made, Mayor Hartsfield and Selznick arrive and join the gathering. Everyone shakes each other's hands as more introductions are made.

The governor invites everyone to sit and make himself comfortable. A colored maid brings a tray of appetizers and places the tray on a side table. She soon returns with another tray that has a pitcher of ice water and a pot of coffee. The maid doesn't speak to anyone, but I do notice that she steals a glance at Samuel. It is a glance of admiration and respect.

With all the introductions complete, the group begins making small talk. Each questions the others about how things have been going and how the weather has been, and I'm questioned about the World's Fair in New York. Everyone listens with interest as I describe details about the fair. Everyone seems to be avoiding the topic that we have come to discuss.

McKinney is the first to bring up the actual purpose of the meeting. When he does, the gathering becomes oddly silent.

McKinney says, "Gentlemen. I know you are very busy with your own endeavors, so I suggest we get right to business with the issue at hand. As the chairman of the NAACP, I have been made aware that the black cast of the great movie of Mr. Selznick's will not be allowed to participate in its premiere here in Atlanta. I was hoping that you may explain why."

The governor and the mayor become quiet, and both begin to fidget in their seats. Selznick begins to answer, but Samuel speaks first. Samuel smiles his caring smile and very softly says, "Forgive me, William, for interrupting, but I, being an old man living in the backwoods of North Carolina, do not hear much about things such as this movie, *Gone with the Wind*. I would like to know what it is about."

Selznick stands, and at first, I think he is going to act out a portion of the movie, but he begins to stroll about the room, all the while telling the story line of the movie. He says, "It's a fictional account of plantation life prior to the Civil War in the South. The story is based on factual historical accounts of that period and begins with the rich and powerful plantations and how eventually they lie in ruin in the aftermath of the Civil War."

Samuel questions Selznick. "Does it depict slavery?"

"Yes, Samuel. As I said, we tried to make it factually representative of that period of history."

"So in this epic movie, there is rape, lashings till people die, the splitting of families, and lynchings of slaves by these plantation owners?"

"Well, no. We could not present it that way. That would not have been appreciated by our audiences."

Samuel stands and strolls around the room himself. Everyone watches him, but he is silent. I begin to wonder if he is going to respond. Then he says, "I was born a slave. My father and mother were both slaves. My experience with slavery was much different than what you present in this movie of yours, but I do understand that your audiences would not be very appreciative of the factual account." The room becomes deathly quiet. As Samuel strolls around the room, he stares at everyone. He continues, "Who are these slaves in your movie? What are their names?"

Selznick says, "Well, there is Hattie McDaniel, who is Mammy the house servant, and Butterfly McQueen as Prissy, another house servant. Oscar Polk is Pork, and Everett Brown is Big Sam; he is the field foreman."

Samuel asks, "And these actors and actresses—did they play their roles well? Did they depict themselves as slaves as you wanted them to?"

"Yes, Samuel. They did a superb job. The director was very pleased with their performance as well as the other cast members. I think they all did a magnificent job, and I expect several will receive Oscar nominations for their performances."

"And what happens if Hattie McDaniel receives a nomination for her performance. What if she wins the acclaim of your audiences and she is given an Oscar? Will she be able to receive this recognition for her effort?"

"Of course, she would be able to receive the award. Nothing would make me, as well as the director, prouder than to see any of the cast receive such distinction for their hard work and dedication."

Samuel smiles and says, "I would very much like to see this movie, *Gone with the Wind*, someday. I think I would find it very interesting to see your perspective on this time of history."

Selznick says, "Yes, I would love for you to see our movie. We must arrange for you to attend this grand premiere."

Samuel smiles and says, "I am so sorry, Mr. Selznick, but under the circumstances, well, we coloreds are not allowed to participate in this premiere. I regret that I will not have the opportunity to view your epic film. If this movie is as great as everyone says it is, it is a tragedy to deny so many in witnessing your great work."

Governor Rivers speaks up and says, "Samuel, I think we can make accommodations for you and a guest to attend this grand premiere. Someone as revered and respected as you deserves the opportunity."

"I am humbled by your invitation and honored that you accept me based on my character and not solely by my color. If you can accept me based on my character, why not Hattie McDaniel, Butterfly McQueen, and the others? They deserve the opportunity much more than I."

"I see your point, Mr. Timmons, but unfortunately, the laws of this state require us to segregate the races. It is for this reason we cannot allow the colored cast members to participate in the premiere. I hope you understand."

"Oh yes, Governor. I understand completely."

The governor looks questioningly at Samuel and says, "Mr. Timmons, I thought you were Cherokee."

Samuel grins, and he glances at me as if to say, "Watch." Samuel replies, "I am a man. A man of many origins and varied, loving relationships. I am proud to be the son of Ezekiel and Sarah Timmons, who were slaves. Proud to be an adopted son of probably the wisest man of all time, Gawonii, a Cherokee. Proud to have been a part of loving families within colored families as well as the Cherokee and proudest to be able to call William here and my good friend Jonathan brothers. You do not show me any disrespect if you recognize me as colored or Cherokee. I am proud of both."

It takes Governor Rivers a moment for everything Samuel said to register, but when it does, he smiles and shakes Samuel's hand. He says, "Yes, I understand as well."

Now that the important business has been discussed, everyone seems to relax, and the small talk and chatting begins once again. Coffee is poured, and we sample the appetizers that were given us.

Selznick is extremely interested in hearing more of Samuel's past, and the two spend the next two hours talking among themselves.

The governor approaches me as he would any other journalist. He is skeptical as to what I might write, but I assure him that I am only there as a friend, a brother of sorts, for Samuel.

I watch William McKinney, and he is talking politics with Mayor Hartsfield. Charles is talking with Selznick, and both are laughing and having a good time with their conversation.

I am amazed at the diplomacy, the strength, and the compassion Samuel exhibited in handling the sensitive topic of the meeting. There is no doubt that each person in attendance was impressed as well.

The governor, the mayor, and Selznick all are clamoring for Samuel's attention. I hear one say, "But what do you think should have been done?" Another one questions, "In your opinion, could this have been avoided?" And then one says, "I must hear more of your story."

I see the colored maid enter and replenish the pot of coffee, and she smiles admirably at Samuel. He stops his discussion with the governor and engages her in conversation. I hear him ask her name.

She says, "Mattie."

Samuel asks where she is from and what her parents' names are. He smiles, and then he escorts her throughout the room, introducing her to each of us. He introduces her to each as if she is of special significance. Everyone, even the governor, shakes her hand and engages her in conversation. The mayor prods her for her opinion on certain issues within the city, and Selznick questions whether she has heard of the movie *Gone with the Wind.*

Mattie becomes the center of attention, and I see Samuel standing at the back of the room smiling.

On the way back to the hotel, once again, McKinney sits in the front seat, and Samuel and I sit in back. I cannot help but question

Samuel. "The thing you did with Mattie. It was nice; it was considerate—but why?"

Samuel smiles and says, "To them, she was a maid. A colored maid. To them, she was a part of the property, not much different than the silver tray she served us with. Once they were awakened to the fact that she was a person—one with a family, a name, a personality—they began to accept her as a person. That was why."

I say, "And is it worth the effort to convince these men that Mattie, a maid, is worthy of their respect?"

"If they can respect and accept Mattie as an equal, then we all have hope."

In the front seat, McKinney says, "I think it was a very successful meeting, thanks to Samuel. I knew you would present our case the way it should be presented. Thank you for participating. By the way, Jonathan, I told Allison I had met one of her acquaintances, and she has insisted we host you and Samuel and of course my good friend Charles to dinner at my house. Nothing elaborate, but I assure you the food will be better than anything you might acquire at any establishment in Atlanta. I think Allison is looking forward to seeing you again, Jonathan." He smiles.

I look at Samuel, and he shrugs. I say, "Only if we can all eat in the same room." Everyone laughs, and we all agree we are to have our dinner at McKinney's.

The drive to William McKinney's house is not that far, and we arrive within thirty minutes. The house is large. It is of the same style as the governor's and almost as impressive, although there are no security guards.

We enter his house and there are no maids, at least any that we can see. Allison greets us in the foyer.

She is more beautiful than I remember, and she smiles graciously at me. I nod, and she approaches me directly and gives me a cordial hug. She says to me, "I was hoping I would see you again."

She then turns her attention to the others and introduces herself to each person.

She grabs her grandfather's hand and escorts the group to the back patio, where huge slabs of ribs are on a grill and cooking. The smell is delicious.

Allison appears to oversee the cooking, but McKinney soon relieves her at the grill. She scurries about bringing drinks and trays of appetizers to our small group. We sit in chairs on the back patio sipping ice tea and enjoying each other's company. I offer to help set the table, but Allison just smiles and says she has it under control.

The food is as McKinney promised. It is delicious. The four of us sit on the patio talking of the day's events. Samuel smokes his corncob pipe, and McKinney smokes his cigarettes. Charles and I converse about his recent graduation from law school. Allison scurries around making sure each have what we need, and then she takes a seat beside me to eat her meal.

I watch Allison listening to the group's discussions, and I notice she appears to be intrigued. She doesn't say anything or join in the conversation. She does lean over to me at one point, and she whispers, "How have you found Samuel to be? Is he as interesting as you might have thought?"

I look at Allison. We both stare into the other's eyes, and I feel there is an attraction. I smile and say, "Yes. He is probably the most interesting and wisest man I have ever met."

She says, "So have you written your story about him yet?"

"No, Allison, I have jotted notes and written a few lines, but I'm finding it difficult to do his story justice. It will take some amazing writing to capture Samuel's story. I'm finding it a formidable task."

She gives me a friendly smile and says, "I must tell you. After I met you on the train, I went to the library and pulled some of the articles you had written for the *New York Times*. I was very impressed with your writing talent. I have no doubt you will do a superb job in telling Samuel's story."

"Thank you, Allison. I needed to hear someone say that."

The evening comes on us suddenly. The darkness consumes our small party on the patio. Allison lights several candles, but the darkness seems to triumph and sends McKinney, Samuel, and Charles indoors. Allison and I sit alone in the dim candlelight.

The sky is clear, and the stars, although not as vivid as the ones I saw a few nights before, fill the sky above. I stare at them, willing them to sing to me as they do Samuel.

Allison sits quietly, staring at the heavens as well. She says, "Do you believe? Do you believe in the cause Samuel and my grandfather are fighting for?" She points to the direction in which McKinney, Samuel, and Charles had retreated.

I say, "I believe in Samuel; that I know for sure."

Allison says, "My grandfather says the same. I wish I knew Samuel as well as you and my grandfather, for I so want to understand, to believe that what they are striving for is attainable. I want to believe in the goodness of mankind."

I put my arm around her, still staring at the skies above. I say, "Samuel once told me, 'Conquer the angry one by not getting angry; conquer the wicked by goodness; conquer the stingy by generosity; and the liar by speaking the truth.' Samuel said that was a quote from something he had read. I thought it was very telling of his character."

She stares at me and then kisses me on the cheek—a timid kiss but warm and full of emotion. She says, "I'm glad I got to see you again, Jonathan."

Charles takes Samuel and me back to the Ellis Hotel, and I retire to my room. I did not bring my typewriter, nor did I bring my dream catcher. I lie on my bed staring at the blank ceiling above me. I hear a few cars passing on the streets below. I think about Allison and how beautiful she is and how sensitive and kind.

I think about Samuel and how he has impressed us all. I think about the mayor, the governor, and the very business-consumed Selznick, and I smile.

The last thing I think of before falling asleep is Mattie.

CHAPTER FIFTEEN

Sometimes war takes an arm, or an eye, or it takes two legs from us, but above all the war takes our belief in humanity away from us!

—Mehmet Murat Ildan

Early the next morning, Charles picks up Samuel and me and drives us back to Glen Choga Lodge in Aquone.

It's a beautiful day, and the ride through the North Georgia mountains is beautiful. We stop and purchase a few sandwiches, which we eat as we ride.

I ask Samuel, "It seems you have spent much of your life seeking equal rights for the colored, but you've not been as active in seeking the same for the Cherokee. I was wondering why."

Samuel begins to tell more of his story.

"I have spent considerable time and effort for my Cherokee people. The hardships and discrimination of Native Americans have not been near as severe as they have been for the colored.

From around 1887 to 1920, the philosophy was to try to assimilate Native Americans into the white society. Land, which the Cherokee had always believed could not be owned, was now being divided into individual parcels of land and deeded to individuals. It was the government's attempt to make the Native Americans whiter. Along with this, the government began to forbid some specific Native Indian practices, such as some of the rituals and ritual dances. They were denounced by the government as paganist. It was around 1920 that I and other Cherokees began to speak out against some of the government's actions.

"Mabel Dodge, an acquaintance from years before, sent me a letter and wanted me to come to New Mexico. She was an artist—and I must say a very good artist. She enjoyed painting the American Indians and scenes associated with their culture. Over the years, I had acquired much of her work, which I have donated to various museums.

"I traveled to New Mexico and helped her gain access to many of the Indian people that she may have not had access to otherwise. While I was there, she introduced me to a gentleman by the name of John Collier. He was white, but he also had a tremendous interest in the culture and history of Native Americans.

"In my discussions with Collier, I learned that he felt that Indians and their culture were threatened by the encroachment of the dominant white culture and policies directed at their assimilation.

"Collier was very intelligent but very outspoken, and this worked against him in many ways. Collier believed that Indian survival was dependent on their retention of land bases. He was against the Dawes Act, which demanded reservation land to be divided into individual household parcels of private property. Some communal lands were kept, but much of the reservation land that did not get allotted ended up as surplus. and the government sold it to private investors. Collier was outraged with this and spoke out quite vehemently against it.

"I personally felt Collier was too outspoken—or, I should say, brash—but I did support his thoughts and ideas concerning the American Indian. I worked with Collier for almost two years, helping him develop a strategy to eventually form the American Indian Defense Association.

"I did not do much in the way of helping John, because he was much more intelligent in the politics of the issue and was much more versed in the legal aspects. What I did help him with was his ability to be willing to understand his opponents. I helped him understand the art of compromise.

"The American Indian Defense Association's purpose was to fight back through legal aid and to lobby for Indian rights. His efforts and studies on these issues raised the visibility of American Indian issues within the federal government.

"Collier was appointed commissioner of Indian affairs by President Roosevelt in 1933. He still is the commissioner, by the way, and I feel has done a superb job.

"The plight of the Cherokee, of all American Indians, was almost the opposite of the plight of the colored.

"The colored wants to be assimilated into white society. They want to have the same rights and the same benefits and share the same responsibility as white society but are denied. Instead they are segregated and refused the same rights as people who are white. It continues to be an issue that the colored fights for.

"The American Indians have almost the opposite problem. The government wants to assimilate them into white society. The government insists the Cherokee live under the same laws and the same culture and live the same as the whites. The Cherokee, the American Indians, do not want this. They want to live as they have in the past. They want the freedom to govern themselves, practice their religious beliefs as they wish, and retain their tribal communities as before.

"Collier, as commissioner of Indian affairs, did eventually convince Congress to pass the New Deal, which allowed the American Indian some self-determination.

"My efforts to help the colored cause centered on trying to convince whites to understand, but my efforts to help the Cherokee cause centered on me trying to convince the Cherokee to understand the whites.

"I will say that I feel the issues that face the American Indian have been much easier to deal with than the issues facing the colored. Please understand that what occurred to the American Indian was horrific. Some might say it was a form of genocide, but over the last sixty years, the whites as well as the federal government have been much more accepting of the Indians and their cultures."

I interrupt Samuel with a question. "I know of the terrible things that were done to the American Indian. I have studied American history and remember the savage attacks on the Indian. Whole communities were uprooted and relocated for no other reason than to steal their land. It was terribly unfair. Do you not feel the need for redemption...revenge?"

Samuel shakes his head no and says, "That's the point, Jonathan. If the Cherokee demanded reparations, sought revenge in some way, all it would do is create a larger gap between the whites and the Indian cultures. At some point, if one wants peace, you must not look back; you must reconcile your differences and walk forward hand in hand."

I think about what Samuel has said. I nod yes, showing I understand. I say, "So in your opinion, you and your Cherokee people have achieved your goals concerning the whites?"

"Not at all. To maintain peace, one must work continuously at it. Continuous conversation between the two must be maintained. This enables trust and fosters a lasting peace."

Not long after lunch, we pull into the long drive of Glen Choga Lodge. It looks the same as we left it two days before. There are a few workers tending to the manicured lawn and pruning a few of the shrubs. A young couple wanders around the pond and then sits beneath a gazebo. They are holding hands, talking, and laughing. They appear to be in love. I wonder if Samuel still longs for Ahyoka. I wonder if, when he sees a young couple so much in love and sharing their dreams for the future with each other, he thinks of Ahyoka and thinks how unfair it was.

I make no mention of the couple.

Samuel and I tell Charles good-bye and watch him drive back down the long drive, the tires of the automobile kicking up clouds of dust. Samuel turns to me and says, "Let's sit on the porch. I want to make sure you understand my views on peace and my views on war. Especially now, when we are faced with the war in Europe."

We sit in the two rockers, and I gaze across the lawn to the young couple in the gazebo. I think about Allison. Samuel begins to explain his view.

"I'm not sure of how much you know or understand of the First World War, but in some ways, this war in Europe that is occurring as we speak is just a continuation of that conflict. Yes, the First World War was fought, and many lives were lost—not to mention the maimed bodies that resulted—and eventually the United States, Great Britain, and France were declared the winners, but the differences were never resolved. The war never resolved anything, other than to bring everyone to the peace table and draw up some ideas. Everyone signed it because they had no choice, at least at that time. The real issues that brought the war in first place were never resolved. Now everyone seems to want to fight about it once again.

"Immediately after the First World War ended, the United States along with the other Allies constructed a peace agreement. It was called the Versailles Treaty. To some this treaty was fair and just, although in my opinion, it was created to punish the Germans. It demanded harsh reparations, which put the German's economy in such disarray as to cause it to collapse. The treaty also redrew Europe's borders, taking over twenty-five thousand square miles and seven million people away from Germany. It required

Germany to recognize the independence of Czechoslovakia, Poland, and Belgium, and the list goes on and on. In effect, the United States, France, and Great Britain won, and they were going to make them pay.

"I understand that to most people, this is just; after all, Germany was the aggressor and in some respects brought all this on themselves due to their greed. But if the purpose of a treaty is to bring peace, especially a lasting peace, then creating a treaty with such demands to punish and to seek harsh reparations primarily for revenge only causes a deeper and more lasting discord. More hatred develops between the parties involved. It has been only twenty years since that treaty was signed, and the discord—the hatred between the people of Germany, France, Great Britain, and the United States—has festered unimpeded. This war in Europe today comes to no surprise to me, but I am terribly saddened.

"I am saddened by the numbers of people that will lose their life, and it will be all for nothing, for regardless who wins on the battlefield, the real war is fought within each of their hearts. That's the battle that must be won.

"I find it frustrating to find that to convince a people to embrace hatred is relatively easy, but to convince the same people to embrace love and compassion is near impossible.

"Jonathan, I have lived beyond what a man should. I am grateful for all these extra years afforded me, but I am deeply saddened that I may see another war, lose more friends, and feel the pain, as I have so many times before. I would have liked to have passed without having to witness such horror again.

"I have grown to like you, Jonathan. I think you are much like me. You are wise, compassionate, and objective in your ideals. That I like about you, but I sense a lack of confidence in you as well. Having self-confidence is difficult for people like me and you. We stand in awe of those who speak so articulately, and wield power with simply their presence. We assume we can never be and we are not the same, but we are, Jonathan. You and I both have that same power, the same presence as those we stand in awe of. We just don't know how to use it. We don't wish to control others, nor do we want to impress others for self-gratification, so we sit silent and begin to lose confidence in our abilities. But that's the point. We have the abilities to effect change. You have the ability to effect change; we need to use it."

I listen to Samuel, and when he speaks so pointedly of my lack of confidence, I want to argue, but I know he is correct. I feel admonished.

Samuel stands and puts his hand on my shoulder. He pats it reassuringly and says, "Gawonii explained the same thing to me almost sixty years ago. I felt the same as you then. In a way, Gawonii gave me his permission to recognize my own power, and I found it liberating. I hope you find it liberating as well."

I stand and hug Samuel. I hug him as a son would his father. My arms surround his withered frame, and the only thing I can say is, "I, too, feel liberated."

Dinner is being served in the dining room, but I insist on eating with Samuel on the back porch as before. I feel I have heard the total of Samuel's story. There is nothing more to tell, nothing more to explain. I have heard the most inspirational and intriguing story of my life, but now I want to simply spend time with my friend.

We sit at the makeshift dinner table made of crates, and the cook, Franklin, delivers a bottle of wine for us to share. There are two candles that light the table; the flames flicker in the soft breeze, casting strange shadows on the cases of produce and crates of fruits that are stacked on either side of where we sit. Samuel lights his corncob pipe and smiles. He says, "I don't imagine you want to try my pipe once again."

I laugh and reply, "No thanks, Samuel. I have never been much of a smoker."

Samuel reaches in his pocket and retrieves another pipe, one that is the same as his. He says, "You do not have to smoke it, but I want you to have it. I fashioned this one the same as mine. The ritual of the pipe is very significant among my people. It symbolizes wisdom, peace, and compassion. It is thought to bring the Great Spirit within us to help give guidance and wellness." Samuel hands me the pipe.

I am honored by his gift and feel regretful that I did not think to acquire a suitable gift for him as well. I say, "Thank you, Samuel. I will treasure this as I treasure our friendship."

We toast and sip our wine.

I look at Samuel and say, "Samuel, I feel I have heard your story, and I appreciate the candor, the honesty, with which it was told. I have a very difficult task ahead of me to capture the spirit with which you told it. I assure you, I will write it to the best of my ability. Is there any part of what you have told me that you wish me not to tell?"

Samuel says, "I have told you everything. I trust your judgment in what should be retold. There is no doubt I have done things I regret; I feel shame for some, but I am willing to take ownership of those mistakes. The story now is yours to tell."

I look at Samuel, and he seems to be studying me in the dim light of the candles. I say, "I must return to New York in the morning. I am having Thomas drive me back to Asheville early so I can catch the afternoon train. I will miss our conversations and the walks. I will never forget this experience. I will never forget you."

"You can always come back, you know. Next time, bring appropriate walking shoes. You might enjoy the walks more." He laughs, as do I.

Our dinner is served, and the cook, Franklin, pulls up a chair beside us. He questions us about the meeting with the mayor of Atlanta, the governor of Georgia, and Selznick. Apparently, it made the news. The cook was interested in hearing more about the movie. He wanted to know what it was about and what stars were in it. Samuel told him the plot of the movie and explained who the cast was. Samuel told the cook about the movie without prejudice. I expected he might suggest that the movie did not portray slavery truthfully, but he did not. He explained it as a movie magazine would have. The cook was excited beyond belief to be talking to two individuals who had such close connections with the movie's production.

Samuel did say, "Franklin, I will tell you, there is one actress—her name is Hattie McDaniel. She is colored. Her performance was so excellent that they are saying she may win an Academy Award. Would that not be the greatest thing of all time? To have a colored receive such an award as that."

The cook says, "Yes, sir, Mr. Samuel. Yes, sir, that would be the greatest thing."

Franklin bows and returns to his kitchen, leaving Samuel and me alone once again. I can hear Franklin in the kitchen, telling his staff about Hattie McDaniel. They all sound overjoyed.

Samuel and I finish our meal and our bottle of wine. I suggest we walk to the pond one last time. There are so many memorable moments I have of Samuel around the pond. I want to be there with him just one more time.

The night is crystal clear. A slight breeze brushes through the stand of hemlock. The cicadas, crickets, and tree frogs create a clamor, but neither of us seems to notice. We walk silently, each consumed with his own thoughts and own emotions.

I ask Samuel, "What did you do with the bugle—the bugle you found in the pond?"

"I debated about that, Jonathan. I considered burying it where Peter is interred, but I was afraid the spirits might still cause him unrest. I'm still not sure how all that works. After giving it some careful consideration, I mailed the bugle, along with a note telling the story of the battle we witnessed, to the Smithsonian Museum in Washington. I wished I could have known the poor bugle boy's descendants. I would have given it to them. The museum was the best I could do. What would you have done with it?"

"Not sure. Knowing me as well as I do, I may have taken lessons and learned to play the damn thing."

Samuel laughs loudly and says, "I tried to blow a few notes myself! It must have disturbed some of the guests in the lodge because Alexander threatened to have me evicted. That's when I decided to send it to the museum."

We both sit in the damp grass beside the pond and laugh. We are like two drunken friends, enjoying a night on the town, yet we each have had only a glass, maybe two, of wine. We are not inebriated with alcohol but with the joy of life and friendship.

I ask Samuel, "May I have some of your tobacco? Your locoweed? I would very much like to try my pipe."

Samuel produces a small pouch and fills the bowl of my pipe. He hands it to me and offers me a match. I light the bowl, inhaling gently. I see the bowl of the pipe turn red. I feel the vapors fill my lungs, and once again I have the urge to cough, but I don't. I exhale smoothly, sending a blue cloud of smoke into the darkness of the night. Samuel laughs.

I feel a peacefulness fall upon me. It may have been the locoweed; it may have been the comradery, the beautiful night that surrounds me, or the Great Spirit entering my soul, but I feel a peace that I have never felt before.

I lay back upon the damp grass and stare at the stars above.

Samuel says, "McKinney's granddaughter appeared to take a liking to you."

"You mean Allison?"

"Yes."

"I really do not know her that well, but I am very fond of her. I hope I can see her again someday."

Samuel says, "You should plan to see her again, Jonathan. Do not leave the possibility of romance to fate."

"Yes, Samuel, I understand."

I find myself staring at the stars above and can sense that Samuel is doing the same. There is a peacefulness that the stars seem to evoke upon me, and that is when I hear their song. It sounds like no instrument I have ever heard. It is almost like a choir, a violin, and a harp, melded into one. I want to tell Samuel that I hear them, but I am afraid I will break the spell. I listen, and the song seems to fill my heart with a joy and a peace that is new to me.

Samuel says, "You hear the stars?"

"Yes, Samuel. I hear the stars."

CHAPTER SIXTEEN

Yesterday brought the beginning, tomorrow brings the end, though somewhere in the middle we became the best of friends.

—Anonymous

Samuel and I sit and talk as old friends. There is no more story to tell other than the incidentals of life. I tell Samuel about my family, my parents, and my college experiences. I think he is impressed; at least, he is intrigued. We talk about Allison and her grandfather, and we even talk about Thomas, my driver and photographer.

I say, "I will miss you, Samuel. The walks, the conversations, and the locoweed, for sure, will be missed, but it's you I will miss the most. I hope this good-bye will not be the end of our friendship."

Samuel smiles and grabs my arm. It's a strong grip. He says, "Friendships are never forgotten, nor are they lessened with time or mortality. They exist forever within one's soul."

I return to my room and pack what few items I have for the trip back to New York. I feel terribly saddened that I will be leaving in the morning. I see the dream catcher and wrap it carefully among my clothes to ensure that it will be preserved. I keep the pipe in my breast pocket as Samuel does.

I begin to write.

The words flow. They are elegant and descriptive, yet there is a bit of vulnerability within, much like I had seen in Samuel. I am overjoyed to find I have the words!

I eventually tire and lie in bed thinking about what I have witnessed and what may come tomorrow.

I awake early. The sun has only been knocking for maybe ten minutes. I have already packed what few items I have, and I go to the dining room to grab a cup of coffee.

Thomas is waiting. He is smiling and seems to be overjoyed that we are finally leaving.

I say, "Well, Thomas, I hope you have the photographs you feel are necessary, because I have my story."

"Yes, Jonathan. I have some great photos."

Thomas drives us back to Asheville. I must say he is driving a little faster than the trip down. I tell him of my experiences with Samuel, and he seems intrigued. He asks questions, and at times he seems bewildered, but I explain, and his interest seems to intensify.

I tell Samuel's story in brief; Thomas questions, and soon we are in Asheville.

Thomas assures me he will send the photographs to the *Times*, and I climb on the train once again.

I sit in my sleeper car and stare out the window at other passengers hurrying across the train platform to board. There are a group of young soldiers preparing to board as well, and I watch them with more curiosity now than I did a week before. Like the others I had seen, they are young and are once again joking, laughing, and carefree. I stand and walk two cars back to help them load their gear onto the train.

I know my help is not really needed, for I know the train's porters will be there to assist them, but for some reason, I feel the need to talk with them. I want to know where they are going and where have they been.

The train porter is loading the duffels onto the train as I arrive at the car. The porter turns and smiles at me as I step forward and say, "Here, let me help you."

The soldiers are climbing on behind their duffels, and as we load the final bag, I stop and stare at the soldier nearest me. He is young—eighteen, I would presume, but he appears to be even younger than that. I doubt the young man has ever had the need to shave. He is smiling. I say, "Hello, soldier. Where are you coming from?"

The young soldier steps further into the car and grabs his duffel bag. He responds, "Coming from Fort Benning. We just finished our infantry training there. Heading to New York."

The young soldier is smiling and is very friendly. I ask, "What are you and the others hearing about the war in Europe?"

The soldier gets a very serious and concerned look and says, "We all think that will be our eventual destination. Not sure how soon though." He smiles again, shoulders his duffel bag, and says to me, "Thanks for your help." And the young soldier disappears down the hallway followed by his friends.

I go back to my sleeper and sit down just as the train blows its whistle and slowly chugs away from the station. I stare out the window, and I see the heavily wooded mountains rising beyond. I see small farms, and occasionally I see a farmer in his field. I watch the scenery pass, but I'm not thinking about the images. I'm thinking about that young soldier and how innocent and vulnerable he appeared.

It's a strange feeling; there is a part of me that is envious of that young soldier, yet there is another part of me that feels sorry for him as well. I wonder how Samuel would explain this dichotomy of emotions.

I envy the young soldier for his bravery, his willingness to put his own life in harm's way to keep others safe. I wish I were that brave. I feel sorrow because I know now that the war and the young soldier's possible death (and those of his friends) may all be in vain. I know now, just as Samuel had said, that the only true and lasting peace is one achieved through understanding and compassion.

I take the corncob pipe from my breast pocket and fill the bowl with a small amount of tobacco. It's not the locoweed that Samuel smoked, for I did not have the taste for it. This tobacco is a common type found in most any market, and is called Sir Walter Raleigh. I find it most enjoyable.

I pull some typewritten papers from my suitcase and begin to peruse them. It is a rough draft of the article I plan to submit to my boss about Samuel. The article is meant only to bring awareness that such a unique person as Samuel exists, for my hopes are that when people read this first article, they will know just enough about the unique persona of Samuel to demand that more be written. My hopes are that the readers will stand by the newsstand each week waiting for another installment about the intriguing Samuel Timmons.

I read the draft and feel pleased. I take a pen and make a few written changes to the draft and then take a piece of stationery out of my suitcase and begin to write a letter to Samuel.

My dear friend Samuel,

I find myself having just boarded the train to New York and already find myself missing your companionship and your inspiring and thoughtful considerations. Thank you for your time, willingness, and honesty in telling me your life's story. I found your story interesting on many levels of conscious consideration and have no doubt that my readers will find it the same. I have completed the first draft of the article I plan to submit and feel very confident that it will be well received by our readers.

I look forward to visiting you again soon, for I truly cherish our friendship and your life's guidance.

Your dear friend,
Jonathan Newcastle

I put the letter in an envelope to be mailed once I arrive in New York.

I sit and stare out the window once again, watching the rolling hills of green, cornfields, and small towns pass by. The train chugs and clanks, and I can see the black smoke from the engine trailing behind, much like it looked a week before, but this time I feel different. I feel happy. I feel important. I feel that my life has a purpose.

I feel I have a purpose, but I have yet to discover it. Equal rights, peace, human rights. Yes, that is it, yet I still have not formulated my own thoughts, my own beliefs, on these topics.

I smoke my pipe.

I smile because I can envision Samuel sitting beside me, thinking, grinning, and having a spectacular interpretation of the thoughts. He is not here, but I sense his presence. He is saying, "I am leaving. I am old. You are now the didanawisgi."

He never said as such, and for sure he never gave me the feeling as if I were to carry his torch, but for some reason I feel it is my torch to carry.

I smoke my pipe.

The porter alerts me that it is time for dinner, and I wander to the dining car, just a few behind. Once again, the dining car is full. The travelers are sitting, chatting, and having a nice time as I look for a place to dine. There is a call—"Hey, come here"—from a grouping of tables in the corner. It is the young soldier that I had met earlier in the day. The young soldier says, "Would you like to join us for dinner?"

"Yes, if you do not mind. I would love to join you."

I settle in between the four soldiers at a table that sits four. They are laughing and enjoying their glasses of beer. I sit, feeling out of place, but I say, "Thank you. There do not appear to be many seats available; sorry to intrude."

The young soldier I had spoken with earlier says, "Please, have a seat. Drink a beer. Have some fun. You never know what comes of tomorrow." And he laughs, as do the others. I sit wondering if I should laugh as well, but I do not. I say, "Thank you for the seat. Yes, I will have a beer, but tomorrow I will have the best story of all time in the *New York Times*."

The four soldiers question me about the article I have written about Samuel. They listen as I tell them a brief sample of Samuel's story. They all seem to be intrigued, and they ask one question after another. I realize that as I tell Samuel's story, I never mention the gold or how it came to be. I do tell them that Samuel became extremely wealthy and that with his wealth, he financed a variety of efforts. Even though the gold and how Samuel obtained it are probably the most fascinating parts of Samuel's story, I for some reason do not feel proper in revealing this part of his life. It may be because I know this part is one about which he has some regret, and I care too much for Samuel to be the one who reveals something that may blemish his reputation.

The soldiers begin telling me about their experiences with infantry training. I listen with interest as they vividly describe their training. I can tell they are proud of their accomplishments, and I tell them I am impressed with their readiness and commitment.

I buy them a beer—well, actually, my boss at the *New York Times* buys the beers, for I tell the waiter to bill it to Harold Sims. I am enjoying the jocularity between the five of us. There are times that we discuss something of a serious nature, and we all offer our individual, serious opinions on the subject; then, two minutes later, someone will tell a joke, and we all share in the humor.

The young soldier I had met earlier in the day, Private Stafford, wants to know if I am going to enlist in the military if we go to war. I say, "Yes, most assuredly. I would hope I could be a war correspondent, writing the details of the war from the battlefield."

They seem pleased that I am willing to do my share. To myself, I am wondering if I would have the courage to put myself in harm's way, but I feel relatively confident that when the time comes, I will be ready.

Private Stafford asks, "Have you written any articles concerning the war in Europe?"

I am embarrassed to tell him, but I do anyway. I say, "No, Private Stafford, I haven't, but I hope to submit an editorial that speaks to the idea of seeking peace. Maybe, just maybe, we can avoid the war altogether. The only way to a lasting peace is through understanding and compassion. War very seldom results in a lasting peace."

The four soldiers become quiet. I can tell they are thinking about what I have just said. They probably want to argue the point. Stafford says, "If someone can convince that maniac Hitler to stop and consider peace, I would be for it. But if he can't understand the idea of peace, then damn it, I'll be more than happy to put a bullet through his head."

The soldiers laugh, but I don't. I say, "I wonder. If war was never an option. If war did not exist. If all we could do to resolve conflicts between one adversary and another was to find a compromise, an understanding of each other. If that was our only option, how many lives would it save, and would not the resulting peace be much more secure?"

The soldiers look at one another and shrug. Stafford says, "It doesn't sound like you will be very willing to participate in the war if it comes to be."

I smile and say, "I prefer to fight for peace, but if I fail, I will fight in battle. I will fight as a mad dog backed into a corner for my life and freedom."

The soldiers nod and smile. The older one of the four slaps me on the back and says, "I know a great infantry school not far from here." Everyone laughs. I don't.

Harold Sims buys another round of beers for our group, and then I shake each of their hands and wish them well. I retreat to my sleeper.

I hang the dream catcher above the small platform bed I have for sleeping. I decide to smoke my pipe and jot a few notes, a few ideas, and the names of the soldiers I have just met. I am determined to follow their whereabouts in the future as best I can, for I feel a need. I feel a brotherhood with these four young soldiers. I find it hard to understand; I have just met these young men. I think I feel this because now I know these four young men personally, and they are friends who may lose their lives in a war that should have been prevented.

I lie thinking, and I realize that these are only four young soldiers I happened to meet. I am disturbed. Then I think about the thousands of other soldiers, the thousands of civilians, their sisters, their mothers, their wives, and God forbid, their children, who will all be affected by this war. I cannot imagine what would bring someone to consider war.

I wish Samuel were here. He would give some elaborate, enlightening statement that would seem to put everything in perspective, but he is not here. I sit here thinking, evaluating, and trying to resolve my unease.

I grow tired—tired of the lengthy travel, tired of the uncomfortable emotions, and tired of the simple discomfort of the train itself. I want to sleep, but I cannot.

I decide to walk to the very back of the train. I stand on the back landing, watching the dark countryside disappear behind me. I am chilled, but I hold the thin metal railing of the landing and try to come to some peace within myself. I look above at the star-filled sky. It's magnificent! I can only imagine what it would be if there were a stillness, a quietness about it, but the train clamors on, screeching, scraping, and rocking back and forth. I smile because even with all the sounds and the motion, I hear the stars.

CHAPTER SEVENTEEN

The humble one is the better one.

—Lik Hock Yap

It is nine o'clock in the morning when the train pulls into Grand Central Station in New York. I feel refreshed, having slept well. I gather my suitcase and typewriter and catch a cab to my office at the *Times* annex on Forty-Third Street. I am extremely excited about what my boss will say about the article I have written about Samuel, although I am a little worried about what his reaction may be concerning the charges I made for the new wardrobe as well as the beer I bought for the young soldiers. If he is upset about the purchases, then I am prepared to reimburse him completely.

Traffic is heavy, and it seems to take forever to drive the short distance to the *Times* annex. I notice as we sit in traffic that there appear to be an abnormal number of servicemen on the streets. The army, marines, and navy are all represented. Everyone seems to be in small groups of three or four individuals, and everyone seems to be having a good time. I wonder if I might see my buddies from the train.

The cab lets me out in front of the *Times,* and I unload my suitcase and typewriter and stroll into the building. I take the elevator to Sims's office on the third floor. I feel nervous. I hope I will be able to maintain my composure and appear confident.

Sims's secretary smiles as I approach her desk. She is about my age; she's attractive, but not overly, and she has always been nice to me. I have often wondered if she was flirting with me on occasion. Today, she just seems to be nice. She says, "Hello, Jonathan. Glad to see you're back. I really want to hear about the meeting you had with Selznick and the movie *Gone with the Wind.*"

I wonder how she knew about the meeting I attended in Atlanta, but I don't ask. I just say, "Nice to be back, Anna. I'll be more than happy to tell you all about it."

Before I can enter Sims's office, he comes bolting out of his office door. He's grinning. He says, "Jonathan, my boy! So glad you are back. I am dying to hear about that meeting with the governor of Georgia and Selznick. Come in and sit. Let's talk."

I shake Sims's hand and step into his office.

Sims takes a seat behind his desk, and with his hand, he gestures for me to sit. He is still smiling. He says, "Ok, Jonathan. I want to hear all about it. I want to hear the story about this Samuel Timmons, and I want to hear about this meeting you had in Atlanta. This may be one of the best stories we have had the opportunity to print in months."

"Yes, sir. It is a great story." I reach into my suitcase and retrieve the article I have written. I tell Sims, "This is the first installment—of many, I hope—of the story about Samuel. It is a most marvelous tale. There is no doubt in my mind that our readers will find it so intriguing that they will be demanding to hear more. Samuel has had relationships with President Grant, Teddy Roosevelt, Woodrow Wilson, and Franklin Roosevelt, not to mention famous entrepreneurs such as Henry Ford, the Wright brothers, and many more. Please read this first article I would like to submit. Of course, with your years of experience, I am anxious to hear your critique of what I have written."

Sims smiles and takes the papers from my hand. He studies them for about ten minutes without saying a word, and then he lays the papers on his desk. His smile is gone, and for a moment I begin to feel sick to my stomach. Sims says, "That's the best article I have ever read. You have outdone yourself, young man. The only thing I will ask of you is to write an article about the meeting you had in Atlanta so that we can print it immediately. Our readers will be most enthusiastic to read more about the movie *Gone with the Wind*. By the way, I hope you will consider traveling back to Atlanta for the premiere. The governor of Georgia contacted me and requested we send you there to cover the events. Jonathan, my boy, I am so pleased."

I say, "Yes, Mr. Sims. I will have an article for you to print concerning our meeting in Atlanta by this afternoon, and yes, I will be more than happy to attend the premiere in Atlanta on behalf of the *Times*."

Sims stands and shakes my hand enthusiastically. He says, "By the way, I got the charge for the clothes and such in Atlanta. I've sent the authorization for payment to accounting. I feel it is the least we can do for you, considering your unselfish sacrifices in capturing these stories."

I walk out of Sims's office feeling better than I have ever felt before. Anna smiles once again as I'm leaving, and she says, "When do I get to hear about the movie?"

I grin and say, "Tonight, if you will accept my invitation for dinner."

"Yes, that would be nice."

On the same floor, I have a small desk, along with maybe ten other journalists. I go to my desk and take out my typewriter and begin working on the article about the meeting in Atlanta. I do not embellish it in any way. I write the story as it had happened, and when I am through, I am amazed at how well it reads. I take the finished article and give it to Anna. I tell her, "Here is the article Mr. Sims requested of me. Please see that he gets it. I am taking off the rest of the afternoon. I have a big date tonight, and I must go and make myself proper." I smile.

Anna blushes and says, "Yes, Jonathan, I will make sure he gets this immediately. May I ask what time I should expect you tonight?"

"Forgive me, Anna. I will come by your apartment at seven o'clock. We can try Antonio's for dinner if you like. That is right down from where you live, is it not?"

"Yes, Jonathan. That sounds magnificent."

I walk out of the *Times* feeling elated. I catch a cab and head to my small apartment in the Bronx.

I take a short nap at my apartment and then shower and shave. I put on my new clothes that I bought in Atlanta and look at myself in the mirror. I look nice. I think Anna will be impressed.

I take a cab to the other side of town where Anna lives. On the way, I think about what has transpired. I am in disbelief at how well my article seemed to be accepted by Sims. I am happy. I want to celebrate, but I do not want to celebrate alone. Anna will be the perfect companion to share in the celebration.

Anna smiles sheepishly when she answers her door. She looks more beautiful than I have ever seen her. She is dressed in a very fashionable blue dress and appears to have tastefully applied just enough makeup to accentuate her natural beauty.

I smile and say, "You look very nice, Anna. I feel privileged to be accompanying someone so beautiful."

Anna blushes and smiles.

It is a beautiful, warm evening, and we walk the two blocks to Antonio's to have dinner. The restaurant is very busy. With the loud chatter of the patrons, the clanging of plates, and the mellow musings of a piano player playing his tunes, I find it difficult to have a conversation. I ask the maître d' if we may have a table in one of the quieter sections of the dining room. He seats us in a cozy alcove, dimly lit with two candles. It is perfect.

We share a bottle of wine and have an excellent dinner. We talk and laugh and have a wonderful time. I tell Anna about my experiences with Samuel and tell her in detail of the meeting with Selznick and the governor of Georgia. She appears to be impressed, although I cannot understand why.

I walk her back to her apartment and thank her for a wonderful evening and say good-bye.

My article about the meeting with Selznick in Atlanta appears in the *Times* the very next day. Sims is ecstatic with it and calls me to his office to congratulate me. He explains that the initial part of Samuel's story will be in Sunday's edition, and they will continue publishing the future installments each Sunday until the full story is told.

Since Sims seems so impressed with my efforts, I decide to appeal to him and express my desire to publish some more editorials. I explain that since my experience with Samuel Timmons, I have felt compelled to write about issues concerning equal rights. I assure him they will be as well received as the articles I had written about Samuel.

Sims is skeptical at first. He questions me about my thoughts and ideas and whom I would need to interview.

I say, "There are many civil rights leaders that I would like to interview: W. E. B. Du Bois, Ella Baker, Phillip Randolph, and many others. I would love to interview many members of Congress to get their perspective as well and maybe even interview the president himself concerning these issues."

Sims sneers and says, "You've got balls, young man. I imagine Roosevelt might be a possibility, since the *Times* has a decent relationship with him, but the others I have no idea about. I think such an undertaking to be foolhardy, but I will allow you to pursue it—but the *Times* will not finance this effort. You'll be on your own as far as expenses. If your effort produces some editorials worth printing, then I will see to it that your expenses be reimbursed. Is that fair enough?"

"Yes. Thank you, Mr. Sims. I will take full responsibility for my finances in this endeavor."

Sims grins and says, "Please realize that you will still be responsible for continuing to write your articles on Samuel Timmons, as well as any news reporting I deem necessary. We do have a paper to run here."

"Of course. I understand completely."

I go to my desk and begin composing a letter to Samuel. I explain to him my desire to interview leaders within the civil-rights movement. I explain briefly in the letter that I also would like to interview members of Congress and possibly the president himself to get their perspectives on the issues of equal and civil rights. My hopes are to create editorials that bring the issue of inequality to everyone's attention and give everyone something to consider. The editorials will be representative of both sides of the discussion and hopefully will ignite objective conversation between people on both sides of the issue.

I request a list of influential leaders he might suggest within the civil-rights movement and humbly request a financial stipend to allow me to pursue these efforts.

I mail the letter immediately and realize I must wait days before I receive a response.

Over the next two weeks, I contact the White House and request to have an interview with the president. The president's press secretary, Stephen Early, questions me about the purpose of the interview and requires me to give him a list of questions I would like the president to respond to. I do so, and within a few days, Early calls me to set a time and place for the interview. I am elated.

The same day I get the call from Stephen Early, I get a telegraph from Samuel. He gives me his approval to help finance my efforts. The telegraph details the arrangement he has constructed. The funds have been deposited in the Georgia National Bank, and the executor of the funds is Allison McKinney. The dispersal of funds will be managed and overseen by her. Samuel says he is proud of my determination to become active in the issue of equal and civil rights for all. He gives me a long list of civil-rights leaders I should contact and gives me his blessing as well.

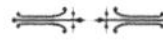

It is June of 1939 before I have the chance to interview President Roosevelt. By then, I have produced seven articles detailing Samuel's story. It has been applauded as one of the best series of editorials that the *Times* has had the privilege to print. With its success comes a little notoriety for myself, allowing me to gain access within the political ranks much easier than before. Everyone, even the president, is intrigued by the story.

In the interview with the president, I ask him the questions I had prepared. He is very candid with his answers. I ask him specifically about the segregation policies of federal employees as well as the federal buildings. He says, "I myself am extremely disappointed in our abilities to treat all men as equals. I personally would very much like to see the colored and the whites work, eat, and live side by side in harmony, but our constituents are not as objective, and it appears all we can do is to continue to negotiate and influence to effect the change we desire. I am afraid it will simply take time for everyone to come to total agreement."

I am surprised to find that he appears to be quite passionate about this, and he seems very interested in my thoughts as well.

I question him further. "Mr. President, as you are aware, the inequality of rights is not only a colored problem. There are Native

Americans, Jewish, and Japanese refugees that are being denied equal rights as well. In your efforts to eventually provide these equal rights, are these people also being considered?"

The president gets a solemn look about him and is quiet for several seconds as he ponders his response. He says, "Thomas Jefferson once said, 'All, too, will bear in mind this sacred principle, that though the will of the majority is in all cases to prevail, that will to be rightful must be reasonable; that the minority possess their equal rights, which equal law must protect, and to violate would be oppression.' I find this statement by Jefferson to be prophetic, and it echoes my sentiments perfectly."

I nod that I understand, and I pursue another line of questioning. I say, "Currently there are only slightly more than three thousand negroes in the army and five black officers, three of whom are chaplains. As fascism grows in Europe, the colored watch with alarm. They particularly object to the racist doctrines of Nazism and are resentful of Hitler's snub of Jesse Owens at the 1936 Berlin Olympics. I understand there may be a military draft, a selective-service system initiated to help man our military. Will this military draft include the drafting of the colored? Will they be inducted as equals or given subservient positions as they were in the First World War?"

The president smiles as if he appreciates my question. He says, "We currently have plans to create two new black units, the 47th and 48th Quartermaster Regiments, and yes, if we institute the selective-service system, then all male citizens of the United States will be considered in the selection. Of course, there will be age restrictions, but race will and should not have any influence on the selection process."

"If the coloreds are to be drafted into the military to fight for our great country, if they are expected to fight and possibly sacrifice their lives so that everyone can enjoy the freedom our country provides, how can one deny them the same rights afforded to the rest? Forgive me, Mr. President; I just have a hard time understanding how anyone can accept this consideration."

Roosevelt smiles once again and says, "Mr. Newcastle, I must say, your questions are much the same as the first lady's. She routinely questions me about these very issues, and I will give you the same answer I give her. Discrimination comes in many forms and has been cultivated within the psyche of society for hundreds of years. A law, an order, a policy cannot be written to erase these prejudices. They must come from within the individual in which they reside. All we can do as faithful Christians is to continue to influence those that do not understand a man is a man, regardless of the color of his skin."

The president requests that I walk with him in the Rose Garden, to which I agree. I ask him a few more questions that I had prepared, and once I was done, he begins to question me about Samuel Timmons. He is most curious about Samuel, and he listens intently as I describe my experiences.

I tell the president about Samuel's philosophy about war. I use much of the same verbiage as Samuel as I press the point about peace. I say, "The only lasting peace is one that is brought about by compassion and understanding of each other."

The president nods in agreement and seems to be contemplating what I have said. He replies, "I would very much like to keep the United States neutral in the war in Europe. That is my immediate concern as we speak."

I explain that his ideas of what he terms the Lend-Lease Policy would eventually involve us in the conflict. Even though it temporarily prevents our soldiers being involved directly, supplying others with weapons and war materials will only include us in the war process, which we should try to avoid.

Roosevelt's response is this: "Jonathan, since 1931, our great country has tried to remain neutral in these conflicts. Unfortunately, we seem to be unable to be isolated in these affairs. If there is no practical alternative, there is certainly no moral one either. We must give aid to our allies, or else their democracies will be extinguished. These philosophies of your friend Samuel are very intriguing to me. He seems to be very wise and prophetic. I would like to meet him someday."

"Yes, Mr. President, he is very wise, and although he has had to endure hardships that most men cannot fathom, he is the most compassionate individual I think I have ever known. You might find it interesting that he has been to the White House on several occasions. He even met with your cousin President Teddy Roosevelt at one time."

"I look forward to reading that part in your story about Samuel," says the president. He laughs out loud, apparently creating an image in his mind of the two sitting around a table discussing issues such as equal rights, peace, and war—Samuel dressed in moccasins, buckskins, and a long, feathered headdress and Teddy Roosevelt dressed in a Rough Riders outfit.

The president walks me back to the White House, and his press secretary, Stephen Early, escorts me out a side entrance to a waiting automobile to take me back to New York.

As I am driven back to New York, I think about the conversation I had with the president. I cannot help but sense his frustration with the dealings of equal rights and the war in Europe. At times during the interview, I found him to be deeply saddened by the issues that we discussed. He seemed to agree that all men should be afforded equal rights, regardless of race, yet there was a hint of conciliatory rhetoric that I cannot ignore. I like the president. He is soft-spoken, yet he speaks with such passion and thoughtful consideration that it rules one's attention. I found him to be deeply concerned with the idea of war. There was no doubt that he would welcome a peaceful resolution rather than waging war, yet I sensed in his demeanor that he had already reconciled within himself that the war was not going to be prevented.

The magnitude of the decisions that the president must make, the torment he must endure, and the responsibility he must feel would be overwhelming for any man to endure, yet he appears to do so with grace and compassion. Yes, I like and admire our president. I make a note to remind myself to write Samuel and tell him I would like to purchase another dream catcher like the one he gave me, for I want to give one to the president as a gift.

In the past, I would have left the president feeling as if I had not succeeded; after all, I did not convince him to consider peace as a possibility or change his thinking about equal rights, but for some reason, I feel as if I did succeed. I imagine it is like Samuel's success with the meeting in Atlanta with Selznick and the others. Neither got what we were after, yet the seed of the idea—the seed of contemplation—was planted both times.

Maybe that was what Samuel was trying to explain to me when I stood beside him at his small garden in Qualla. He had said, "I find such pleasure in sinking my hands into the soil of the earth, planting the seeds, and feeling what the new season might bring."

The seeds are being planted. Now I too will see what the new season might bring.

CHAPTER EIGHTEEN

So it's true, when all is said and done, grief is the price we pay for love.

—E. A. Bucchianeri

I continue submitting installments of Samuel's story to the *Times.* Each week another part of the story appears in the paper, and it has become a topic of much discussion. Every day when I am on the subway, I see countless people reading the article. I overhear them discussing the story, and I feel a sense of pride swell within me.

Just the content of Samuel's story is enough to capture an audience and evoke discussions of differing opinions. Anyone with only a small amount of literary skill could have written the story and had enormous success; the story itself captures the people's emotions. But I had poured my heart into every word and every sentence, and I had created what some had termed a masterpiece. I wanted the readers to enjoy it, but I was more concerned with making Samuel proud.

I ask Anna, Sims's secretary, if she would be kind enough to send a copy of each article about Samuel to Private Joseph Stafford, of the 82nd Armored Reconnaissance Battalion. I tell her I know they were in New York, at least for a while. She assures me that she will take care of it.

Private Stafford is the soldier I had sat with on the train coming back from North Carolina. I think sending regular installments of my articles to him might allow me to keep track of where he and the others are. I think of them often.

My boss, Sims, has kept me extremely busy, and the assignments are some of the most important. I feel extremely grateful for the opportunities that are handed me, but I now feel more empowered to seek the stories I feel compelled to write.

At one time, I considered myself a reporter, a journalist who reported interesting happenings. I had felt it my duty to tell these news stories in an interesting and grammatically correct nature, but now I realize that not only do I report, but I can also effect change. I now involve myself within the stories I report, and by so doing I can influence opinions. It is most gratifying to realize I can effect a change of sentiment.

In July, two months after my visit to Aquone, I called Allison McKinney and requested a small amount of the money from Samuel to help finance a trip to Los Angeles, California. I wanted to interview a prominent civil-rights leader named Betty Hill. Betty Hill's Women's Republican Study Club was one of the more vocal clubs. It not only sought to promote African-Americans and fight racial discrimination, but it also fought against the New Deal and policies that were collectivist and advanced the cause of the Republican Party. Being a realist, however, after the mass migration of African-Americans from the Republican to the Democratic Party in the 1930s, she changed the name to the Women's Political Study Club.

I figure if I am traveling to Los Angeles to interview Betty Hill, then I might as well interview Hattie McDaniel too. There are grumblings from the colored communities that Hattie McDaniel had acquiesced to Hollywood's stereotypes, providing fuel for critics of those who were fighting for black civil rights.

Betty Hill and Hattie McDaniel have very different opinions on how best to achieve equal rights. Betty Hill is very outspoken and is considered by most to be very confrontational when it comes to her efforts to acquire equal rights and eliminate discrimination. McDaniel, on the other hand, takes an approach like Samuel Timmons. She develops relationships with the white majority, works hard, and wins their respect and feels that this is the best way to achieve equality and eliminate racial discrimination. I am looking forward to hearing both of their ideas on the topic of equal rights and how best to achieve harmony.

Allison responds that the funds would be available—but only if she can join me. Apparently, Betty Hill is a hero of hers, and she wants to meet her. I am in no position to argue. I say, "Of course."

Allison arrives in New York two days before we are to leave for Los Angeles. I am excited to see her but am a little uneasy as to what her role in accompanying me is to be. With just the few discussions I have had with Allison, I realize she is very opinionated about equal rights. One might even consider her an activist, much like me. I figure that is the very reason Samuel had put her in charge of the funds. He had wanted her to be involved with my efforts—and possibly be involved with me as well.

I light my corncob pipe and wait on the platform as the train begins to unload. I see her step off the train. She is more beautiful than I remember. A porter is helping her with her luggage; he puts it on a cart and whistles for assistance from one of the station porters. She sees me and waves enthusiastically.

She gives me a friendly hug and says, "It is so good to see you again, Jonathan. I am so looking forward to our travel to Los Angeles. I have never been to California; have you?"

I shake my head sheepishly, for I have never traveled west of the Mississippi before. I say, "No, Allison. Never been to California, but I am looking forward to hearing Miss Hill's perspective on equal rights. You look very nice, Allison. I remember you being beautiful—just not this beautiful."

She blushes and says, "Thank you. You are kind." She glances at me and says, "I like your pipe. Is that the one that Samuel made for you?"

"Yes, Samuel gave this to me. I never was a smoker before, but I have developed a liking for it. When I smoke the pipe, I feel I am communing with my old friend." I laugh an almost-silent chuckle. We walk toward the exit with the station's porter and Allison's luggage in tow. I say, "I have a taxi waiting outside to carry you to your hotel. The Waldorf is only a few blocks away. Shall we go?"

"Yes. That would be nice. I would like to freshen up before our meeting with Jane later."

I say, "Jane? Jane who?"

Allison says, "I'm sorry. I must not have told you. Jane Bolin."

I knew of Jane Bolin. She is a successful New York lawyer and is being considered by Mayor La Guardia to be appointed as judge of the domestic-relations court. It has been in the news and is rather controversial; I have not involved myself either professionally or personally in the controversy. I say to Allison, "I know of Jane Bolin. What does your meeting with her concern?"

Allison grins and says, "She is a very good friend of mine. I met her a few years back when she had just graduated from law school at Yale. Did you know she was the first black woman to graduate from Yale's law school?"

I shake my head no.

Allison continues, "My grandfather tried to get her to move to Atlanta. He wanted her to lead the NAACP. Unfortunately, Jane wanted to continue living in New York and work at her father's law firm, which she did. The word is that now she is being considered to be appointed a judge. When I told her I was coming to New York, she insisted we meet and have dinner. Kind of a precelebration. Nothing official, just friends celebrating."

I realize that I had made reservations for two at Bull & Bear Steakhouse, thinking Allison would want to dine with me. I say, "Oh, I wish I had known. I had hoped you would join me for dinner."

Allison grins and says, "Jonathan, I am so sorry I didn't tell you. My friend Jane wants both of us to join her for dinner. She has been reading your articles about Samuel, and she is dying to meet you."

I say, "I would love to join the two of you for dinner."

The taxi drops the two of us at the Waldorf, and the bellboys scurry about loading Allison's luggage onto carts; they carry them to her room. Allison turns to me and says, "I must take a nap and freshen up a bit. I think we are to be at Oscar's Waldorf at seven o'clock."

I say, "Oscar's is here at the hotel. A beautiful dining experience. I will be here at seven."

Allison grins and kisses my cheek. She smiles and says, "Thank you, Jonathan."

I take the taxi to my apartment and try to nap as well.

I arrive at the Waldorf at 6:30 p.m., much too early, but in New York, you never know how long it may take you to get where you are going. I decide to have a glass of wine at the bar of the hotel, and I smoke my pipe. There is a *New York Times* lying on top of the bar, and I think about reading it. I have not completed my daily reading of it yet.

Instead, I let my mind wander. I think about Allison. I wonder if she is as attracted to me as I am to her. I remember the first time I met her on the train and how I was impressed with her simplistic beauty. It's more than her beauty though. She has an air of class, a regalness of sorts, that one cannot help but notice. I am curious as to how the meeting between Allison and Jane Bolin will be. Allison said they were good friends, so will the meeting be just two friends getting together over dinner, or is there more to Allison's agenda? I wonder what the real reason is for my being invited. Is Jane Bolin truly impressed with the story about Samuel, or are there other reasons for me being included?

There is a tap on my shoulder, and I turn to see a young gentleman standing behind me. He smiles and says, "Excuse me, sir, sorry to interrupt, but I was wondering if you might be the journalist with the *Times*? Jonathan Newcastle?"

I return his smile and study his face. I have never met him before. I say, "Yes, I'm Jonathan Newcastle."

The young gentleman says, "I thought I recognized you from a few of the photos with Samuel Timmons. I just wanted to let you know that I have been very impressed with Samuel's story. I find it quite remarkable. You must be very proud to have had the opportunity to meet someone as interesting as Samuel Timmons. I find your writing abilities superb."

I stand and shake the young man's hand. He might be a few years older than me but not many. I say, "Thank you for your gracious compliment. I must admit I am very proud to have met Samuel and even more proud to be able to call him a good friend. Excuse me for my rudeness. What is your name?"

"Sorry, how rude of me. I'm John Steinbeck. I'm an author as well. I have just published *The Grapes of Wrath*. By chance, have you heard of it?"

I am astounded! Now that he has told me who he is, I recognize him. I feel so stupid. I say, "Most definitely! Not only have I heard it, but I have read most of your works. I have not read *The Grapes of Wrath* yet, but I plan to do so. I am such a big fan of yours, Mr. Steinbeck."

He reaches in a briefcase at his side and withdraws a hardback copy of *The Grapes of Wrath*. He says, "I would be honored if you would accept this book as my token of gratitude for your brilliant story about Samuel."

"Most definitely, Mr. Steinbeck. Please, if you do not mind, will you sign it for me?"

Steinbeck smiles and takes a pen from his front coat pocket and writes a quite lengthy paragraph within the front cover. He hands the book to me and says, "You should write novels. You are most talented, Mr. Newcastle."

He turns and strolls out of the bar.

I glance at my watch, and it is 6:55 p.m., so I walk into the lobby of the hotel to find Allison.

In the middle of the lobby, there is a beautiful grand piano. A pianist is playing some classical melodies, which I recognize, but I cannot think of their names. I see Allison sitting in one of the large, plush chairs facing the piano. She is listening intently. She looks beautiful.

I approach and say, "Are you fond of the piano?"

"Yes. I love the piano. I could sit and listen to this all night. He is very talented!"

I say, "I think it is about the time we are to meet your friend Jane. Shall we go to the dining room?"

"Yes, of course." She stands, and I offer her my arm as we walk toward the main dining room. As we walk, Allison notices the book underneath my other arm, and she asks me, "Is that a book?"

I nod yes and say, "I arrived early, so I sat in the bar and had a glass of wine. John Steinbeck recognized me from my story about Samuel and we had a small chat. He gave me his latest book."

She looks at me in wonderment and says, "Mercy, Jonathan. You sure get around."

The maître d' takes us to our table, and Jane Bolin has already been seated. She stands and hugs Allison. I can immediately tell they are good friends. Jane then turns her attention to me and shakes my hand. She introduces herself, and I do as well. She says,

"Mr. Newcastle, I have been so impressed with your story about Samuel Timmons. Allison and I have been friends for quite some time, and when she told me she knew you, well, I'm sorry; I insisted she introduce you to me. I really hope you will tell me about your experiences with Samuel over dinner."

"Yes, Ms. Bolin, my good friend Samuel Timmons is my favorite topic to discuss."

"Please, Mr. Newcastle, call me Jane."

"Yes, Jane, and please, call me Jonathan."

I would guess that Jane is about ten years older than Allison, but she is a strikingly beautiful black woman. She is dressed in a fashionable, navy-blue business suit and carries herself with a manner that some might consider arrogant, yet when she speaks, there is sincerity and compassion that comes forth. I listen to the two friends banter as friends do.

Over dinner, we sip our wine, and Jane changes the subject and begins to discuss Samuel. She asks me questions, one after the other, about Samuel's character. She seems well versed in Samuel's history but seems overly inquisitive about his personality, his motivating factors, and his personal feelings about segregation versus integration.

I like Jane. I can understand why she is being appointed as a judge. She is very inquisitive and appears to study every word and thought of others before speaking and giving her own thoughts on the issue being discussed.

I question Jane about the possibility of her being appointed judge of domestic-relations court, and she explains. "I would very much welcome the opportunity to preside over the court of domestic relations. To judge on issues concerning such an important part of society—families, children, and their relationships—is to judge on the most basic foundation on which everything else is dependent. How can society ever hope to prosper if the family has no tenability? I look forward to confronting the issues on the domestic front, taking great care to the plights of children. Segregationist policies that are now entrenched in the system, including skin-color-based assignments for probation officers and social workers, must be changed. That is what I feel I can do. That is what I must do."

I nod and say, "I agree completely. I think you would make a wonderful choice for a judge. The people of New York will benefit greatly to have someone like you helping in those most important issues."

The three of us sit and talk long after we finish our dinner. We order two more bottles of wine, and we enjoy our conversation about business, politics, equal rights, and the impending war. Jane questions me about my trip to Los Angeles and what I hope to accomplish.

I say, "I want to learn, to understand Miss Hill's thoughts and motivations. I will listen as she explains, and hopefully I will be able to explain my thoughts as well. If I can plant an idea, a thought, in her mind as to the benefits of accepting the idea of conciliation, then I will feel it is a successful trip."

Jane looks at me as if amused. She says, "Jonathan, she will never understand. You are white. She will never accept the idea of compromise, especially from you. What she asks for, what she works for, is simple recognition as an equal. How can she compromise being considered your equal? There should be no compromise."

I smile and respond, "I understand, but I feel as involved in the quest as her. Will she not understand my impetus?"

Jane grins and nods. "I admire your dedication to such ideals. Is this what Samuel aspires to as well?"

"Yes, most assuredly."

Jane says, "Then I understand your passion."

I explain further about the intent of the trip. "Not only will I interview Betty Hill, but I will interview Hattie McDaniel as well. As you are probably aware, Miss Hill and Miss McDaniel have very different opinions on how best to achieve equal rights and eliminate discrimination. Hopefully, after listening to both of their opinions on the subject, I will be able to write an objective editorial on the subject of racial discrimination and equal rights for all people."

Jane studies me, measuring how truthful she believes me to be. She smiles and says, "And my opinion on equal rights and racial discrimination—will you write about them as well?"

I take a moment, give her a very serious look, and say, "Only if you allow me. I will never write a word about someone without first obtaining their approval. Please, Jane, understand that Betty Hill's interview, Hattie McDaniel's interview, and eventually scores of other interviews will only make me more informed on the issues people are facing. My editorials will simply be my personal feelings on the subject and will hopefully provide some truthful information for my readers to ponder. I once asked Samuel if he was a negro. Samuel pounded his chest and told me to look deep, deep inside his soul, and he then asked me what I saw. I told him I saw a kind man. I hope you, Betty Hill, Hattie McDaniel, and all of my readers will consider my soul as well—because that is the motivation of the words I write, not the color of my skin."

Jane smiles and grabs my hands across the table. She says, "Well said, Jonathan. I was already a fan of yours, but I am even more so now."

The conversation changes once again to the things friends talk about. Jane and Allison discuss the newest fashions and what is going on in each of their personal lives. Jane asks Allison whether she is dating anyone, and I notice she blushes noticeably but shakes her head no. Allison says, "I'm afraid that I am too plain for most men, not to mention that I can be very opinionated. Plain and opinionated do not attract many suitors." And she laughs, as does Jane.

I interject, without thinking. "To me, you are extraordinarily beautiful. Maybe a little opinionated, but—"

Both Jane and Allison laugh hysterically at my admission. I turn red with embarrassment and sink lower in my chair. I know they are not laughing to be malicious or teasing, yet I am terribly embarrassed. Allison grabs my hand under the table and squeezes it gently. Between bouts of laughter, she says, "Jonathan, that is the sweetest thing I have ever been told." She continues laughing and squeezes my hand reassuringly.

The three of us leave the dining room together and walk out the front door of the lobby. A taxi is hailed, and Jane hugs Allison, shakes my hand, and says, "Allison, it is always so nice to see you. You are a dear friend, as are you, Jonathan. I hope to see the two of you much more often. See you soon." And she climbs into her taxi and leaves.

Allison and I walk back into the hotel and decide to have a cocktail at the bar. It seems much darker in the bar than it had been earlier in the evening. There are candles placed about, which provide most of the illumination. There is a piano player playing romantic melodies in the corner. We sit in a small booth opposite the room from the piano. There are only two or three other patrons in the bar. One gentleman sits by himself at the bar, sipping his whiskey, and another, older couple sits at a small table adjacent to the piano. A waiter approaches and takes our order.

The wine is poured in our glasses, and we both take minute sips, not because we are unsure of its palpability but because we both desire to make the moment last. I watch Allison take her sip. The candlelight flickers and dances around her face. The soft light accentuates her dark-brown curls that barely touch her shoulders. She smiles, and her blue eyes sparkle in the warm glow of the candle. I want to tell her once again how beautiful she is, but I choose to bathe in the silence and the emotions that seem to swell.

She also sits silent and toys with her glass of wine. She seems to be thinking, contemplating, and dancing with the emotions that seem to fill the space between us. She speaks first and does so most timidly. “This song that is playing is my favorite. It is so beautiful. Is it not?”

I nod yes.

Conspiratorially, Allison asks, “Would it be inappropriate for us to dance?”

I stand and offer my hand. There is no dance floor, only a small space between the tables. Fortunately, there are no other patrons who may be offended. We embrace and begin a slow, rhythmic sway to the beautiful melody. Allison rests her head upon my shoulder, and the beautiful melody seems to fade as our sentiments swell. I begin to dance—not to the song but to the passion that seems to fill us both. We drift about the small space afforded us, yet there is nothing else within our senses other than our emotions. Allison timidly caresses the back of my neck as we sway. Our eyes meet occasionally in the dim light, and we realize we both feel the same way. Neither of us speak for fear of spoiling the moment. We dance to the beating of our hearts.

CHAPTER NINETEEN

There is never a time or place for true love. It happens accidentally, in a heartbeat, in a single flashing, throbbing moment.

—Sarah Dessen

Allison and I board the Twentieth Century Limited, an express train to Chicago, at 6:00 p.m. the following evening. It is a luxurious train with private Pullman sleepers, and the patrons are literally given the red-carpet treatment. A red carpet is rolled out to board the passengers in New York, and the same is provided on arriving in Chicago. It is a delightful experience.

We arrive in Chicago the following morning around 9:00 a.m. Once again, the red carpet is rolled out as we disembark the train and take a taxi to the Stevens Hotel.

There has been little discussion between Allison and me concerning the very emotional time we had together in New York. I personally am not sure what to say, and for some reason I feel she is confused as well. We approach each other as friends with a secret we don't want to admit, yet we both seem to treasure the memory.

We check into the Stevens Hotel, a luxurious hotel on Michigan Avenue. It is by far the largest hotel I have ever been in. Both Allison and I are amazed by the magnificent grandeur of the lobby.

I have an appointment with Earl Dickerson at 4:00 p.m. at Chicago's city hall. Earl Dickerson is a colored attorney of some distinction. He has been an active leader in the politics of Chicago as well as a leader in civil rights. He has just recently been elected to Chicago's city council, the city's first negro council member. In the planning of our trip to Los Angeles, I had realized that we would have a layover in Chicago and thought this would be a perfect opportunity to interview Dickerson. I am most interested to hear his opinion on integration and equal rights.

After hearing my plans for the afternoon, Allison insists on joining me in the interview. She promises she would not interfere; she just wants to watch and listen. She describes her participation as being a fly on the wall.

Allison and I have lunch at a café within the hotel. We find a small table for two at the far end of the café, which allows a bit of privacy. I review my notes about Earl Dickerson and prepare several questions I intend to ask him. I go over these with Allison, and she seems intrigued.

Allison says, "Jonathan, I am so impressed with your interviewing skills. You have some very pointed questions prepared. Have you met Mr. Dickerson before?"

"Thanks for the compliment. No, I have never met Dickerson before. I have read many articles about him though, so I feel as if I know him."

"Jonathan, I have been reluctant to mention anything about our moment at the Waldorf in New York. You know, the dancing. I hope I was not too forward in asking you to dance. I realize we should keep ourselves professional; after all, this is a very important business trip for you and for me as well. The music, the ambience, everything was so beautiful—I just could not resist. I want you to know that I am sorry if I stepped out of line."

I look up from the papers before me and smile. I hold out my hand and take Allison's hand. I say, "There is nothing to apologize for, Allison. It was one of the most beautiful moments of my life. I feel I should be the one apologizing for my lack of dancing abilities."

Allison laughs and says, "Not at all, Jonathan. I was rather impressed with your dancing."

"Maybe we can do it again soon. Practice makes perfect."

Allison blushes. Nervously, she grabs her purse and retrieves a small mirror and pretends to be checking the condition of her makeup. I think she is merely trying to hide her flushing face.

I say, "We should probably find a taxi and head over to city hall. I would not want to keep Mr. Dickerson waiting."

Allison and I arrive at city hall in plenty of time. At first, we think that we might just mill around a bit since we're so early, but a receptionist insists that Mr. Dickerson is not busy and can see us at once.

The interview goes well. Dickerson's rhetoric is one of an attorney. Everything he attempts to explain is riddled with legal jargon. He refers to past legal judgments to explain his opinion. He says things such as "That is best explained by the Lovell vs. Griffin ruling of the Supreme Court." At this point, I stop him and ask that he explain in layman's terms, which he does.

I ask him a question that I had not prepared. "Of everything you have accomplished, what are you most proud of?"

"In the war, I was a lieutenant and served in the American Expeditionary Forces in France. After the war ended, I helped form the American Legion, a federally chartered corporation that formed a brotherhood of sorts for all veterans. I think I am most proud of that."

I cannot resist my next unprepared question. I ask, "With war on the brink in Europe as we speak, may I ask what are your thoughts concerning that?"

"I saw too much death, too much pain and loss, in the last war to ever agree to be a part of another. There is no good that comes from war."

I shake Mr. Dickerson's hand, and Allison and I gather our belongings and prepare to leave. Mr. Dickerson stops me and says, "May I ask you a question, Mr. Newcastle?"

"Yes, of course, Mr. Dickerson." I turn and wait for his question.

He says, "How is my friend Samuel doing? I have not seen him in many years, and with his age—well, I am most concerned for his health. Please understand, he is a dear friend of mine as well."

I smile and take out my corncob pipe. I light it and say, "He can still outwalk me. He is doing well despite his 101 years. I will tell him you asked about him. That will make him proud."

I have the concierge at the hotel secure a reservation for Allison and me in the Oak Room, which is the finest dining room on the hotel's premises. The Oak Room is known for the famous patrons that dine there. Every president since 1927 has dined there as well as many of the world's leaders. Famous actors and actresses are routinely seen in the Oak Room. I am excited to experience such a famous establishment.

The Oak Room is elaborate. The expansive dining room hosts hundreds of tables draped in fine white linen. Fresh flowers in brass vases sit upon each table, which are set with only the finest china, crystal, and silverware. The ceilings are appointed with bronze and crystal chandeliers and feature original fresco-style oil paintings. They are beautiful beyond words. The walls are draped with Venetian curtains, each with murals that give the room warmth and elegance. Most of the tables are seated with guests; most I would assume to be of some importance, yet as we are guided to our table, I do not recognize anyone.

Allison sits and smiles demurely. She says, "My, my, Jonathan. This is a most special place." She looks around the room studying the faces, hoping to recognize someone famous. She gets a surprised look on her face and turns to me, exclaiming, "Jonathan, I think that is Katharine Hepburn sitting at the far table to our right. Don't make yourself look obvious, but look. I'm sure it's her!"

I casually glance around the room and spot the table that Allison has mentioned. I grin and say, "I believe you are right. If that's not Hepburn, then it most assuredly is her twin sister." Another lady and two gentlemen sit with Hepburn, but they do not appear familiar.

I order a bottle of Chateau Mont-Redon wine, and we sip the luxurious red. Neither of us can keep from searching the room for another famous face. Occasionally, I glance at Allison as she glances around the room, and I realize that each subsequent time I see her, she seems to be more beautiful than the last. There is a time or two she glances at me as well, and our eyes meet. For that moment, there seems to be a warmth that ripples between us. It swells as if a gentle tide, a tide of sentiments that teases the desires within us both, a rolling emotion that whispers at the other's heart.

Our dinner is a remarkable experience. The presentation of each dish is such that one regrets destroying the beauty. The taste is strange, exotic, and most delightful. Allison and I talk. We talk about her parents and her childhood. She asks me about mine. I discover that her parents are extremely wealthy, spending most of their time now in Europe. She explains to me that she never knew them well. They were always traveling, usually separately, and she was usually left in the care of her grandfather. I sense there may be some resentment toward her parents for their neglect.

I tell her about my childhood, which is bland. My father was a postman and my mother a housewife in one of the poorer sections of the Bronx. Allison asks me, "What made you decide to be a journalist?"

"I loved to read. I read everything I could get my hands on. To me, reading was my escape."

"And what did you read? Who were your favorite authors?"

I do not have to even contemplate the question; I say, "F. Scott Fitzgerald is my favorite; then there are Hemingway and Mark Twain."

Allison says, "So you decided to write yourself. Maybe become a novelist?"

"No, nothing like that. I felt there was power with words. I was inspired by these authors, and I felt the power they seemed to have. I wanted to experience that ability to influence others through writing. Does that sound pompous?"

Allison studies me for a moment and then says, "Not at all, Jonathan. I am impressed. Fitzgerald was my favorite as well."

After dinner, Allison and I decide to leave the hotel and walk about Michigan Avenue to see the sights that Chicago has to offer. It is a pleasant evening, warm for Chicago, and the skies are clear. We pass a small bar tucked away a few blocks from the hotel. We hear music coming from the dimly lit establishment. We stop and listen for a bit and decide to step inside. The bar is filled. At the far end of the small room, there is a band, and right away I recognize the performer. It is Louis Armstrong. He has his trumpet in his left hand, and in his well-known raspy, bluesy voice, he is singing "All of Me."

There is a small dance floor directly in front of the small stage, and several patrons are taking advantage of it and swaying to the jazzy tune the band is playing. I look at Allison and say, "Shall we practice our dance skills?"

Allison laughs and nods yes. I take her hand and escort her through the crowd to the dance floor. We embrace lightly and begin our rhythmic steps to the tune. Allison smiles and pulls me a little closer to her. It may have been because the small dance floor was rather crowded, but I hope it is because she simply desires to be held.

We dance several songs, and there are a few times Allison rests her head on my chest as she had done in New York and seems to melt within my embrace.

It is getting late, so we reluctantly leave the small lounge and walk back toward the Stevens hotel. This time, though, we walk hand in hand.

I have the strong desire to tell Allison that I am falling for her, that my feelings are becoming much more amorous, but I can't seem to find the right words. We walk in silence, and I debate about what to say. I wonder if she is debating the same. I think about what Samuel had told me—to not leave the possibility of romance to fate.

I say, "Allison, I hesitate to tell you this for fear that it might seem improper, or at the least complicate our friendship, but I must admit that I am growing very fond of you. I realize we have a professional relationship and I think a wonderful friendship, and I would never want to jeopardize that, but I am finding it difficult to only think of you as just a friend. Sorry I'm bringing it up like this; I just know no other way than to be up front with you."

Allison stops and turns toward me. She stares at me for a moment with a look of surprise and I fear I may have over spoken. She smiles and says, "That is very sweet, Jonathan. I too have similar feelings and have been reluctant to admit it to you and maybe even myself, for I have always seen you to be on a mission in life. A mission that left little time to share with anyone. I accepted this about you, but I cannot prevent the feelings I am having."

I pull Allison close to me and wrap my arms around her. We stare at each other a moment, searching each other's eyes for validation, and then I timidly kiss her. It is a soft kiss; my lips barely touch hers. It is a kiss of coyness, yet it is facile and full of emotion.

Allison whispers, almost breathless, "Oh, Jonathan, what are we to do?"

Back at the hotel, I kiss Allison good night and go to my room to try to get some rest, for we have another long train ride the next day.

I find it hard to sleep. I keep thinking about Allison and our newly discovered relationship. I find it extremely exciting to be able to share my thoughts, my emotions, and my innermost secrets with someone like Allison and not have the fear of being judged wrongly. I can't help but feel valued for Allison to be so forthright with me about the dysfunctional relationship she had, and apparently still has, with her parents. Her honesty about such a personal issue makes me realize that when one begins to love another, the need to reveal one's personal weaknesses feels necessary. For if someone can accept you for what you are—your strengths and weaknesses—then love becomes a possibility.

It is very late, and I know I should sleep, but I am unable. I open the curtains, which allows some of the light from the street below to bend its way into my room. Strange shadows dance across the ceiling, and the muted sounds of car horns, people talking, and the general hustle and bustle of late-night Chicago creeps into the room, attempting to disturb my dreamlike thoughts about Allison. Even with the distractions, I revel in the warmth and comfort I feel with knowing that Allison and I do have a chance. A chance at love.

Somehow, I sense Samuel is staring at the stars, hearing them sing and realizing that Allison and I are falling in love.

I begin to hear the stars, and I fall into a deep sleep and dream of Allison.

The next morning, we board the train once again and head toward Los Angeles to meet with Bettie Hill and Hattie McDaniel. It will be a day and a half of travel before we finally arrive in Los Angeles. Normally, I would be disturbed by the idea of being on a train for almost two days, but since I will be spending this time with Allison, I don't seem to mind.

Over the next day and a half, I spend almost every minute with Allison. I am surprised that she involves herself with my assignment. We go over my notes and together come up with questions to ask Betty Hill and Hattie McDaniel. I am impressed with Allison's interest in these matters. I soon come to realize that she is as devoted to the cause as Samuel and me.

We spend hours discussing the politics of racial discrimination and equal rights. I find her to be extremely intelligent and very sensitive to the plight of the colored. I find this strange since she was raised in a very wealthy white family in the South. I question Allison about this, and she smiles and explains. "Jonathan, please remember, I was raised by my grandfather William McKinney. I simply assumed his ideas and beliefs, and now I have come to believe in your goals as well."

Allison and I stay busy with work and conversation, but when dinner approaches, our discussion changes. We begin to discuss ourselves, our desires, and our emotions. There is an electric aura that seems to fill the space between us. We whisper our thoughts as if there is someone that would care to hear our amorous murmurings.

It may have been the soft whisperings or the slight, accidental touches, or maybe it was Allison's eyes—something brought me to the realization that I was falling in love. There is a moment of silence, and we are searching each other's eyes, both of us wrestling with overflowing emotions and with what we want to say. Allison smiles and says, "Yes, me too, Jonathan."

CHAPTER TWENTY

Success usually comes to those who are too busy to be looking for it.

—Henry David Thoreau

In Los Angeles, Allison and I meet with Hattie McDaniel and Betty Hill. We meet with them on separate occasions, for I realize they are very different in their beliefs as well as their concerns about equal rights. I find Betty Hill to be very intelligent yet very abrasive in her attempts to explain her plight. It may be because I am white that she feels compelled to batter me with accusations of not being sincere: "After all, what do you know personally about discrimination? Have you ever been denied access to a restaurant, a school, or a restroom?"

I try to explain that even though I never had the misfortune to experience what she describes, I, as a human, can understand the wrong. That is why I feel dedicated in searching out people like her to help me understand so that I can bring the information to others.

She never seems to want the interview to end. She continues ranting and raving about all the inequalities afforded to the colored, and all I can do is agree.

Hattie McDaniel is almost the opposite. I am astonished when she tells me that Clark Gable will be joining us in the interview. He has threatened to not attend the premiere in Atlanta in protest of Hattie's exclusion. She insists that he participate in our interview so as he might come to the realization about what is best for all.

Allison, of course, is with me during both interviews, and I cannot help but notice her swoon in the company of Gable. I don't think he is intentionally flirting with Allison. I think it is his character, an image he feels he must project, that causes him to smile coyly. A handshake that seems to linger too long or the way he positions himself purposely to sit beside her during the interview. Whatever the reasoning of all the nuances, I realize that Gable handles himself as a complete gentleman. I am impressed with his concern for Hattie and his regret that Hattie will not participate in the premiere, although when Hattie explains how she is fine with the decision, Gable nods his head as if he understands.

Gable stands and shakes my hand; he nods and smiles at Allison. He turns toward Hattie and hugs her as a son would hug his mother. It is a loving hug, full of compassion and emotion. He whispers something to her, but is not for our ears. I can only assume what is said.

Allison and I take our notes and our observations and board a train to Atlanta.

It takes four days for us to finally make the journey back to Atlanta, and it is a wonderful four days. Our relationship grows exponentially, although neither of us seem willing to admit we are falling in love.

In Atlanta, we go to the NAACP headquarters, where Allison's grandfather is hard at work. I have written several different articles concerning equal rights based on the interviews I have already had and of course my own ideas on the subject as well. He reads the rough drafts and smiles appreciatively. I can tell he is impressed with my efforts.

McKinney sets the papers down and takes on a look of seriousness. He slowly begins to tell Allison and me some disturbing news. He says, "Jonathan, I know how much you care about Samuel. A couple of days ago, I received a message from some of the people he is close to in North Carolina. Apparently, he had some sort of stroke. He was hospitalized in Asheville, but yesterday, I arranged to have him brought to Grady Hospital here in Atlanta. He will get much better care here, and well…at least there are people here to be by his side."

"How is he? Is he going to be all right?" I question, very disturbed

"Yes. As of this morning, Samuel was awake and seemed to be doing much better. He was asking about you."

"I should go see him as soon as possible. Will they allow me in to see him?"

McKinney smiles and nods yes. He says, "I'll have Charles drive you over to the hospital."

"Thank you, William. I should go at once then, if that is all right?"

Allison grabs my arm and says, "Jonathan, I'll go with you."

"Thanks, Allison. We should leave now before it gets too late."

We are escorted out the back entrance of the office complex by Charles, and we climb into the automobile. He drives us to the hospital.

The staff at the hospital asks who I am and what my relationship to Samuel Timmons is. I answer, telling them I am a close friend. The staff finds my name on a list of people whom Samuel has authorized to see him, but unfortunately Allison's name is not included. Allison says she will wait in the lobby of the hospital and insists I go ahead and see my good friend.

When I walk into the room, Samuel smiles and waves me to sit beside his bed. I say, "What has happened, my friend?"

Samuel grins and says, "Who knows? I fell or passed out or something while I was walking, and now they are all up in arms, as if something is wrong. It's not like it hasn't happened before."

I look at Samuel, and even though he is trying to be funny, he does not look to be in good health. Nothing like I last remember him. I say, "Samuel, you must do what they say. I know you are in great health. You can outwalk me most any day, but you are getting up there in age. Maybe you should start taking it a little easy."

Samuel looks as if he is about to question my reasoning and then says, "Do you have your pipe?"

"Yes."

"Let's have a smoke. If you don't mind me sharing yours. They took mine away from me."

I pull my pipe from my breast pocket and start to fill the bowl with my tobacco. I stop and say, "Sorry, Samuel, I only have the tobacco that I prefer."

Samuel waves his hand as if he is disgusted and says, "Look over there in my coat pocket. The left one. You will find the locoweed I prefer. I think we both could use some."

I dig around in his canvas jacket and find the leather pouch that contains his cherished herb. I fill the bowl of my pipe with the stringy leafage and light it with a strike of a match.

Samuel smiles and says, "I taught you well, my son."

I cough slightly and hand the pipe to Samuel. He says, "I am glad I am able to see you again, for there are a few things I must explain to you in more detail than I had before."

"Sure, Samuel. What?"

Samuel takes a puff and hands the pipe back to me. He seems to think a moment and then says, "You'll learn as you get older that life and life's order can be rather complex. There are many things that may present themselves, and sometimes there may be no right or wrong answer. Sometimes you may have to take a very unpopular stance on a subject because it is the right thing to do, and it may result in many people or groups of people turning against you. During the time I spent with you, I tried to enlighten you to some of the most critical ideologies of life. Unfortunately, I may have led you to believe that these ideologies are exact and true. They are not. Do you understand what I am trying to tell you?"

"I do, Samuel, but why do you tell me this now?"

Samuel seems to reposition himself in his bed and then says, "You have become like a son to me, a son I never had. Please humor me and listen, for I have much to say."

I pull up a chair.

Samuel begins to explain. "The story I told is all true. The principles I spoke of are true as well, yet there are other thoughts to be considered, and these are what I feel I must discuss with you. These considerations are most complex, but I will try to explain. First, please understand that I am a firm believer that all people, regardless of race, color, or creed should have equal rights. Everyone should be afforded the same rights as the other, in my opinion. But please understand that this does not mean all men are equal. There will always be some that deal in evil, and they will work to destroy the decency and good found in others. Even these evil ones deserve equal rights, but never should they be treated as an equal. Equal rights may be legislated, yet respect and acceptance as an equal must be earned by the individual. One of the most upsetting aspects of my plight to achieve equal rights for all is that it has been turned upside down by some, colored people as well as whites, who feel that they should be given the same respect and acceptance without first earning it. Remember, equal rights can and should be legislated, but it is up to every individual to command their equal stature in life."

Samuel stops and takes another puff of my pipe and stares at me to make sure I understand. I nod for him to continue.

"There will be many that believe the same as you on many subjects yet will have very different ways to approach the same problem. I think you may have already discovered this with your recent interviews with Betty Hill and Hattie McDaniel. I knew this about them for some time now and hope I did not mislead you to believe that everyone would present the same solution to the problem of inequality. Neither Betty Hill nor Hattie McDaniel is wrong, and neither is completely right, yet even though they appear on the surface as complete opposites, it is with people like these that you can achieve the most advances, because they desire and strive for the same result. They just differ as to how it is to be done. I had this problem with Booker T. and Du Bois. They were different as night and day, yet they wanted to achieve the same thing. It is most important to understand their differences and embrace each. A wise man will intercede and bring the differing opinions to a common understanding. It can be very frustrating at times.

"We had long discussions concerning war and peace, of which I tend to be very opinionated. I am afraid I gave you false hope in achieving lasting world peace merely through compassion and understanding. I personally believe that if all mankind accepted the idea of working with the other to achieve peace, the world would be a much better place. Unfortunately, as I said previously, there are those that deal with evil and will work diligently to thwart one's attempts at peace. Knowing there are those that are evil should not prevent you from dedicating yourself to the goal, which is peace. Peace through compassion and understanding. If one stands tall and pronounces this ideology, then one by one, the others will begin to listen and slowly begin to accept it. If you begin to perorate the idea that there may be exceptions, then everyone will begin to consider their individual exceptions, and peace will almost be impossible to achieve. That is why I told you there was almost never a legitimate reason to choose war over peace.

"I had tried to describe my love for Ahyoka while telling my story. I hope I impressed upon you the extent of that love, for I loved her beyond belief. When I lost her, I think part of my very soul was lost as well. When it comes to love, I told you to not leave it to fate, and I still believe that to be true. But I feel you should know that once you commit yourself to another, and you accept their commitment of love for you, then you begin to have an enormous responsibility toward each other. I feel I failed in my commitment to Ahyoka. Even though we were told we could not marry, there was still that commitment of love between us, and I failed to be there for her. I will always regret that mistake.

"Lastly, I want you to understand how proud I am to be able to call you a friend. I know I have lived well past my time, and I know my time here on earth is short. Therefore, I feel a need to impart to you as much wisdom as I can, for I know now that you were brought into my life for a reason. You are like me; you have a ravenous hunger for understanding these complexities of life, and we also have the same desire to impart what we have come to understand to others. I think this a very admirable quality, yet I was never able to write or speak my understandings as eloquently as you."

I nod at Samuel and say, "Thank you for the compliment, but I fear you may have overstated my abilities and virtues."

Samuel smiles and continues to lecture. "When my adopted Cherokee father, Gawonii, began to prepare me to become didanawisgi, he told me that he recognized the hunger to understand in me and began to impart his wisdom. He told me I was chosen to become didanawisgi. I remember that I laughed. I asked him how I could. I was not even a real Cherokee, nor did I have the wisdom necessary. How could someone of my abilities accept such an important position? Gawonii explained that the Great Spirit chooses the didanawisgi. The Great Spirit knows who is capable and gives those chosen the abilities necessary to fulfill their duties. The Great Spirit has told me you are to assume the position of didanawisgi. With the same way I was brought into Gawonii's life and chosen to be didanawisgi, you were brought into mine."

I look at Samuel with a look of shock. I say, "Samuel, that is absurd. I feel very privileged to have been the recipient of your wisdom and will always treasure that knowledge and our friendship, but there is nothing about me that qualifies me to be didanawisgi. I am not like you. I am just a normal man that has no abilities other than to write someone else's wise ideas and ideologies. I am flattered that you think I am capable, but I am not."

Samuel smiles and takes my hand in his rough, wrinkled hand. He grasps it tightly and says, "I am sorry, Jonathan, but like me, you do not have a choice. You are didanawisgi, whether you accept it or not. I did not have a choice either. Your only choice is to either be a good didanawisgi or a bad one. That is your choice. I hope you will do as I did and choose to be the best you can be."

I stare into Samuel's dark eyes and see the same spark, the same love of life, that I had noticed the first day I met him. Even though his body has withered with age and is failing him, his spirit is as alive as ever. I feel his compassion and his understanding. I say, "I will do the best I can, Samuel."

Samuel lets go of my hand, and, smiling, says, "I have read your articles about me. I am impressed with your skill. I hope your readers have found them to be interesting."

"Yes, the readers seem to be very intrigued by your story," I reply, but I am still thinking about the conversation about didanawisgi. I feel that Samuel has gotten off his chest what he had felt necessary and now wants to change the subject. I decide to humor him and say, "I still have several more installments before it will be done. I am glad you approve of the articles."

Samuel takes another puff of the pipe and then hands it to me. He says, "I hope you didn't mind me taking the liberty of putting Allison McKinney in charge of the trust I set up for you. She is a very bright lady with a lot of promise within the workings of the NAACP. I think she will do an excellent job. Do you agree?"

It is my turn to smile now, for I know Samuel is fishing for information. I say, "Yes, I think she will do a magnificent job. I have become very fond of her. I think we will be seeing a lot more of each other soon. I must thank you for being so enterprising in appointing her as the executor. It was an excellent choice."

A nurse comes into the room and gives Samuel and me a dirty look, for she smells the smoke and the terrible odor from the pipe. She opens the window and waves her hand, gathering the fumes and waving them out the window. She remarks, "Please, Mr. Newcastle, you must not smoke in this room. Poor Mr. Timmons is a very sick man. This will only make his condition worse."

I nod and say, "Forgive me. How thoughtless of me." I look at Samuel and say with a wink, "Sorry, Samuel, please forgive me for smoking."

Samuel begins to tell me what the physicians have told him of his health and prognosis. They seem to think he may have had a mild stroke but feel he should recover almost completely. There seems to be a lingering weakness in his right leg, and occasionally, he has severe episodes of dizziness. The physicians had said they hoped these episodes of dizziness may disappear in time, but until then, they prefer that he use a wheelchair.

I have a good visit with Samuel, and I bid him farewell. I tell him I plan to stay in Atlanta for the next few days and will stop in to see him every day. I explain that I will be back in December for the *Gone with the Wind* premiere and hope he would be fully recovered by then.

I find Allison still sitting in the lobby. She is reading the book given to me by Steinbeck. I say, "Is that *The Grapes of Wrath* you're reading?"

She smiles and marks her place in the book with a piece of ribbon. She says, "Yes, and thank you for loaning it to me. It is most interesting. How was Samuel? Is he going to be all right?"

I nod and say, "He seems to be doing fairly well. I mean, what can one expect of someone over a hundred years old? He has had a mild stroke and has been instructed to move about by wheelchair, at least for a while. I need to get to the hotel and freshen up a bit before dinner."

Allison had already asked me to come to her house for dinner. She had said that her grandfather was going out of town and she would have the house to herself. She wanted to fix me a true Southern dinner—fried chicken, collard greens, mashed potatoes, and sweet tea. I don't think I had ever had collard greens, and even though I'd had iced tea on many occasions while traveling in the South, I was accustomed to sweetening the beverage myself. I felt sure Allison knew what she was doing, and I was looking forward to spending some alone time with her, not only to continue our affectionate musings but also to share more of my earlier discussion with Samuel.

I was still a little bewildered by the conversation with Samuel, especially the idea that I was to be didanawisgi. Possibly, Samuel was beginning to show signs of senility, or it could be lingering effects from the stroke that made him to not think clearly. Whichever it was, I felt the need to discuss it with someone. I knew Allison would give me some understanding.

That evening after dinner, I begin to elaborate on the conversation I'd had with Samuel earlier. She listens intently yet is a little amused. She questions, "And what are the duties of didanawisgi?"

"Mary, mother of Jesus, Allison! I have no clue! That's the point: how can I be the one chosen when I don't even know what it entails?"

Allison smiles and grabs my hand in hers. With a very caring tone in her voice, she says, "You should ask Samuel about these concerns, these questions. You are a dear friend to him, and he would not want to impart any undue stress. I'm personally ok with dating a didanawisgi—if you don't have to wear a feathered headdress and war paint!" Allison laughs hysterically, and I do as well.

CHAPTER TWENTY-ONE

There is only one way to happiness and that is to cease worrying about things which are beyond the power of our will.

—Epictetus

I have several conversations with Samuel over the next several days. I end up staying two weeks in Atlanta. I continue writing my articles and sending them to Harold Sims on a regular schedule. The editorials and stories were being well received by the readers, and Sims had even mentioned that the *Times* had seen a definite increase in circulation since my articles began to be published.

Maybe it was being around Allison those two weeks, or possibly it was the deep conversations and time I spent with Samuel, but by the end of the two weeks, I surprise myself and decided to move from New York to Atlanta. I discuss this with Sims, and he seems fine with the idea if I can continue to write and send the articles for publishing on a timely schedule.

My duties as a journalist have changed dramatically. I've gone from a simple news journalist who reported newsworthy happenings to writing thought-provoking and entertaining editorials. I can write these articles almost anywhere, so I decide to move to Atlanta to be with Allison and be closer to Samuel.

Samuel is still unable to move about without the use of a wheelchair, for he is still having the dizzy spells. On occasion, if the weather is nice, I push Samuel in his wheelchair and visit some of the parks that surround the hospital grounds. Samuel seems to enjoy these walks immensely, and as we wander through the park, he once again begins to enlighten me on the complexities of the world. I have come to the realization that he is not senile, nor is he mentally diminished due to the stroke. He explains quite adequately everything I had a question about. I find him to be even more amazing than I had thought previously.

When I question him about the absurdity of me assuming the role of didanawisgi, he responds, "It's like a husband that is told his wife is to have a child. Sometimes the husband wants to be a father; sometimes he may feel a little inadequate to assume the role. Regardless of how he feels about it, the Great Spirit has decided to make him a father. It is up to the husband to decide how good a father he is to be. The Great Spirit has decided you are to be didanawisgi, and who knows? The Great Spirit may decide to make you a father someday as well. You have so much to be delighted for."

There are a couple of times that Allison accompanies us to the park, and even though Samuel converses with her equally, I recognize that the conversations that Samuel and I have when alone are much more ethereal. I do not mention this difference to Allison, for I fear she might feel somewhat slighted. She has grown to love Samuel as much as I do, and I was proud to consider them both my friends. I will admit that Allison's and my relationship has become much more than a simple friendship. We both realize that we are romantically involved, and we begin to openly admit our courtship to others in our social circle.

I find a small two-bedroom house not far from the NAACP headquarters; I rent it and arrange to have my few belongings moved from New York.

After four weeks in the hospital, Samuel is finally released, but it has been recommended that he move into an assisted-living facility close to the hospital and his physicians just in case there is a medical emergency. Allison and I help make the arrangements and move him into the facility at the end of September.

Samuel has only been there for two or three weeks when he voices his dislike of the place to me. He tells me the staff is friendly and seems to be attentive to his needs, but he misses his home. He misses the mountains, the streams, and his Cherokee people. He wants to go home.

Allison and I borrow her grandfather's automobile, load Samuel's belongings, and drive him back to his home at Qualla town in North Carolina.

It is only a few hours' drive from Atlanta to Qualla town, and it is a beautiful drive. Fall progresses much more rapidly north of Atlanta, and we discover that in the higher elevations, the leaves are at peak color. Cascades of colors—reds, oranges, and bright yellows—blanket the mountainsides, and at every curve a new, awe-inspiring view seems to overwhelm us.

We get Samuel settled into his house at Qualla, and Allison and I decide to stay at Glen Choga for a few days, just to be close to Samuel and to help him get things in order. Under Samuel's direction, I harvest what is left in his meager garden, and both Allison and I help build a ramp to his porch to allow him to wheel himself in and out of the house. Even though it is a lot of work—manual labor, which I am not accustomed to—it is fun. Samuel supervises the work, making wisecracks along the way, which keep Allison and me laughing. By day's end, we have the ramp completed, the garden harvested, and the house straightened and cleaned.

Samuel insists on cooking dinner for us. As he begins gathering the materials and the ingredients from his pantry, he starts to explain. "I would like for you to experience a traditional Cherokee dinner. You will find it most unique and delicious. I do want you to try it, but I'm really making it because I've longed for a familiar meal."

Allison and I look at each other and shrug. I say, "Sounds good to me. But please let Allison and I help you."

Samuel gathers the ingredients and begins to explain what each is. There are venison, winter green onions, sautéed *wisi* (a type of mushroom), cornmeal and crawdad mush, and squirrel gravy. The raw ingredients and Samuel's explanation of each of them begin to kill my appetite, and I think Allison feels the same, but we continue with the process of helping Samuel prepare the meal. As the ingredients begin to cook—some in the oven, some on top the stove—there is a savory aroma that fills the room, and our appetites return; we are more ravenous than before.

It is well past dark when the dinner is complete, and we set a mismatch of plates, bowls, and glasses on the small dinette. The only lights provided in the room are a couple of kerosene lamps and an occasional candle. It is a delightful experience to behold.

Samuel is smiling broadly, looking much happier than he has in the last few weeks. I assume it is because he is home, somewhere that is familiar to him, a place that holds many fond memories. The soft, flickering of light from the candles casts eerie shadows across the room. Samuel's long, unkempt white hair and beard make him look like a ghost in the flickering light.

Samuel lights his pipe and offers me his pouch of locoweed. I accept it and light my pipe as well. He seems to study me for a few moments and then says, "I must apologize to the both of you in advance, for I have just recently received some troubling news that demands immediate attention. Therefore, I must interrupt our pleasant evening and our friendly conversation to discuss these most important happenings."

Both Allison and I nod for him to continue. I suddenly feel an intense uneasiness, for I have never seen Samuel so serious, with such concern in his words. Samuel takes another long drag on his pipe and then begins to explain.

"At this very moment, there is a ship off the coast of Cuba. It is the *MS St. Louis,* and it sits in the Havana harbor with a little over nine hundred Jewish refugees from Germany. These refugees have been promised temporary refuge in Cuba until their immigration applications can be processed by the United States. Unfortunately, the Cuban government, under political pressures, has now rescinded its initial decision to accept these refugees and will not allow them to disembark. The ship and its passengers may be forced to return to Germany, where these nine hundred Jews will surely be killed or, at the very least, imprisoned."

I nod and say, "Yes, I have read a little about this in the newspaper. I don't know all of the details, but I am aware of this."

Samuel continues, "The JDC—better known as the Joint Distribution Committee, which is one of the organizations that I have chosen to help fund—has taken on the task of trying to resolve this issue. Lawrence Berender, the JDC's leading attorney, is currently on his way to Havana to intervene and hopefully broker a deal with President Federico Laredo Brú of Cuba to allow these refugees to disembark. I only bring this up now because of the extreme urgency of the situation. In the past, with something of this importance and urgency, I would be personally involved in trying to resolve the dilemma. Unfortunately, my health prevents it now. My dear Jonathan, I feel this predicament deserves our personal attention. I humbly request you join Mr. Berender on my behalf and help solve this crisis."

I am stunned and speechless as well. A tremendous feeling of panic overwhelms me, and apparently, Samuel is aware of my trepidation. He continues to beseech me with his reasoning before I can refuse. He says, "Please listen to me, Jonathan. I was a runaway slave, a refugee of sorts myself once. If the Cherokee had not intervened, I would not have survived. It took Peter to involve himself in my troubles to save me. Would you have denied helping me then?"

I squirm in my seat, and I feel Allison staring at me. I feel flushed, and I'm still at a loss for words. I glance at Samuel, and he smiles a comforting smile. I say, "I would hope I would have done everything possible, even risking my own life, to save yours, Samuel."

Samuel gives an affirmative nod.

I say, "When should I leave?"

CHAPTER TWENTY-FOUR

Our frustration is greater when we have much and want more than when we have nothing and want some. We are less dissatisfied when we lack many things than when we seem to lack but one thing.

—Eric Hoffer

It takes me three days to get to Havana. Lawrence Berender had arrived a day before me, and he fills me in on all the issues that we face in trying to get the Cuban government to allow the passengers to disembark. It is much more of a mess than I had ever considered.

The Cuban government's position is that the landing certificates have been sold illegally and that Cuba must insist upon strict adherence to its laws. Furthermore, Cuba has admitted a greater number of refugees proportionately than richer nations. The government neglects to mention that the arrival of the *St. Louis* coincides with a wave of anti-Semitism in the Cuban press, radio, and

Congress, together with a fierce rivalry among pro- and antigovernment forces over the millions of dollars that might be extracted from desperate refugees.

Berender has arranged a meeting with President Brú, although we are told that he has already demanded that the *St. Louis* leave the harbor the next day. The JDC has acquired $125,000 to offer as a bond for the Cuban government to help in the temporary settling of the Jewish refugees in Cuba. Both Berender and I feel that these funds might eliminate the government's reluctance to allow the disembarkation of the refugees.

Our hopes are soon dismissed when the president tells us his mind has already been made up. Even though he sympathizes with the refugees, he feels he must stand his ground and demand the ship leave the harbor. There is a tremendous amount of political pressure being applied on him from the people of Cuba and other government officials.

Both Berender and I are devastated. We can see the ship in the harbor and see hundreds of the Jews standing along the railings of the ocean liner, hoping and praying they were not going to be turned away.

Late in the afternoon, Berender and I are taken aboard the *St. Louis* to inform the passengers of our failure to convince the Cuban government to allow their disembarkation. It is probably the saddest moment of my life. Many of the refugees cry openly, and some scream for us to please help them and not to let them be turned away. They hold their children in their arms, and I can see helplessness and fear in each of their eyes. I feel as if I have failed them as well as Samuel.

Berender and I leave the ship in a cloud of frustration and despondency. I ask Berender, "Can we not contact our government? Can we not try to get President Roosevelt to allow them temporary asylum?"

Berender says, "We can try, although there are strict laws governing immigration into the States. From what I've been told, the number of immigrants for this year has already been surpassed. It will be nearly impossible to convince the president to use an executive order to allow them asylum, especially since 85 percent of Americans are against it. But we'll try."

We send a cable to President Roosevelt requesting his consideration of the matter. We describe in detail the seriousness of the situation. If the refugees are not given asylum, then they will have to return to Germany and probably to their deaths.

Roosevelt does not bother to even respond to our petition.

The next day, the *St. Louis* sets sail out of Havana harbor heading back to Hamburg, Germany.

As Berender and I are planning to leave Cuba, we hear rumors that President Brú had offered to accept those refugees who would pay him $500,000. Hearing this sickens both Berender and me as we realize that there are those who are so greedy and heartless.

Berender travels back to New York, and I go back to Atlanta. Both of us are saddened, frustrated, and feeling as if we failed.

Immediately after returning to Atlanta, I write a lengthy editorial describing what had happened in Havana. I send the article to Sims at the *Times*. Two days later, Sims calls me and says that he cannot put the editorial about the Jewish refugees in the paper. In his words, "It is a too controversial topic to print now."

Not only have I failed to help convince either Cuba or the United States to accept the Jewish refugees, but I also have failed to get the story published to make everyone aware of the atrocity.

I feel I am a terrible failure and reluctantly call Samuel to give him the sorrowful news.

Samuel says, "You did what you could, Jonathan. You can never expect to win every battle. All you can ever do is fight for what you know is right. I am proud of you for trying."

Even though I have failed miserably helping the Jews of the *St. Louis*, Allison treats me as if I am a hero. I describe to her in detail what Berender and I did to help save the refugees. I tell her about our efforts to convince Roosevelt to allow a temporary settlement of the Jews and how he never responded. I let her read the editorial I had submitted to Sims for printing, and as she finishes reading the article, she cries uncontrollably for the poor souls who were returned to Germany.

Several days after I return to Atlanta, I receive a phone call from President Roosevelt. He said, "Jonathan, I wanted to let you know that I am still following the story you continue to print in the *New York Times* about Samuel. I am terribly moved by his story and applaud you for the meaningful way it is told. I also wanted to express my sincerest apology for not responding to your request concerning the refugees aboard the *St. Louis* in Havana. I am deeply saddened that we could not resolve such a horrific situation for our fellow man. Please accept my apology. I will always feel a deep sense of guilt in this matter."

I am silent for quite a while as I listen to the president's apology. I feel an anger rise within me and want to berate him for his lack of will, but I sense Samuel's whisper in my ear. I say, "I understand your sensitive position concerning the Jewish refugees and their situation. Unfortunately, I will always remember their stares and pleas for help till the day I die. I too am sorry."

After a couple of weeks, Sims contacts me and says that if I will rewrite the article concerning the Jewish refugees and simply tell the facts, leaving out all the political opinions and observations, then he would love to print the story. I rewrite the story telling the refugee's plight, but I leave out the failures of the Cuban government as well as the failures of our own government in resolving the issue. I read it one last time before mailing it and decide to toss it in the wastebasket, for it is nothing but a lie.

Anna calls me several days later and says Sims is still waiting on the article about the Jewish refugees. I tell her, "Tell him I am not a fiction writer; I am a journalist. If he wants the story, then he must accept the true and complete story. Tell him I'm sorry."

Sims calls me himself within an hour, and he is furious. He says, "Damn it, young man! You write what we want you to write. You write for me! If you do not produce an acceptable article concerning the situation that occurred in Havana, then the expenses incurred will not be paid by the *New York Times*."

I respond, "If the *New York Times* wishes to publish and profit on my writings, then they are welcome to do so, but they will always be *my* writings. Please do not concern yourself with the expenses of my mission to save 930 fellow members of mankind. The expense has already been paid for by my dear friend Samuel Timmons."

Sims is quiet for several moments, and I am expecting him to say, "You're fired!" But he doesn't. He gets a soft tone in his voice, almost as if he understands, and then he says, "Very well, Jonathan. I will try my best to convince the people upstairs to let me publish your original article concerning the refugees."

I say, "Thank you, Harold. I understand the article will make many uncomfortable, for there are those that are complacent, misinformed, and simply greedy, but they too must share in the guilt of sending over nine hundred people to their deaths."

The next week, my original editorial is published.

I am elated as well as surprised to see it printed, for I know it is very controversial politically, yet I know the story should be told. I know there will be some who will be angered. There will be others who will be embarrassed into silence, and then there will be a few to stand up and applaud my attempt to expose the lack courage of those in power to come to the defense of the oppressed.

It turns out that the article draws an almost equal number of positive versus negative reviews. Every radio station in the United States references my article in its daily discussions. It creates such a stir within the populace that the *Times*' circulation increases dramatically. Once again, I am summoned to New York to receive an award.

Allison accompanies me to New York for the award. We have dinner with Jane Bolin, Allison's friend, the first night. She has just been appointed judge of the domestic-relations court, and they both seem to enjoy the time together. The second night is the night I receive my award. It is quite elaborate. The ballroom is filled with people of importance. Almost every state and city official is in attendance as well as several members of the US Congress. What surprises me is that the actual award is presented by a Jewish rabbi. His name is Harry Katzen, and he is the rabbi of Congregation Beth Israel West Side Jewish Center. His presentation of the award is eloquent and emotionally moving. When he hands the plaque to me, I look him in the eye, and at that moment, I see the same pleading stare, the same cry for help, that I had witnessed a few weeks prior on the *St. Louis.* I whisper to him as I take the plaque, "I'm so sorry. I did what I could."

He smiles and says, "That is all any of us can do. You are a good man. You should be proud."

I did invite my parents to this event, and I am surprised that they show. I think they are surprised and proud to see that I am held in such high regard. I get to introduce Allison to them following the award ceremony, and the four of us spend a couple of hours celebrating afterward. Both of my parents voice their opinion on the issue of the Jewish refugees, and it comes as no surprise to me that theirs is the opposite of mine. I do not argue the point, for they did take the time to read the article, and that is all I can ask. I have begun to realize that I cannot always change people's minds. I cannot always make someone think and feel the same as me. I can only give him or her the information and my thoughts to ponder. I tell them, "I am glad you read the article. I wish I had the pictures of the mothers holding their children, pleading for mercy, for they knew they were being sent to their death. The pictures would have told the story better."

My parents hug me and say once again how proud they are of me. They hug Allison and say how we need to get together more often, and then they leave. I watch as my parents hold hands and walk away.

While Allison and I are in New York, I stop by the *New York Times* and meet with Harold Sims. I am surprised that he humbles himself and apologizes for not printing the editorial about the refugees right away. He explains that the higher-ups were a little worried to print such an inflammatory article, but now with the success and the amount of publicity that followed the article's publishing, he is being praised by his superiors for his insistence that it be printed. He says, "Thank you, Jonathan, for your perseverance and for allowing me to share in your success."

Anna, Sims's secretary, gives me a bundle of mail that has recently arrived addressed to me. There is a letter from John Steinbeck praising me for such a poignant editorial concerning the Jewish refugees. There are many letters from people I do not know: Frank Weinberger, Jonathan Cohen, and many others, names that I would assume to be Jewish. They praise the article and my attempts to help the refugees in Cuba. Several of the letters bring me to tears, for there are a few letters from family members of some of the refugees who had been on board the *St. Louis.*

There is one letter from Private Joseph Stafford. I realize right away that he was the young soldier I met on the train from Asheville. He is the one whom I'd had Anna send each article I wrote. He thanks me for taking the time to send the articles and hopes that I will continue, for good reads are hard to come by for him.

Allison and I take a plane back to Atlanta the next day. We talk all the way back about all the events that have occurred over the last few days. She says, "You seem to have really made a name for yourself. You should be very proud."

"Any success I might achieve will be due to Samuel and his influence. I will always be indebted to him for enlightening me in so many ways."

Allison rests her head on my shoulder and says, "Samuel is a great man. He has touched many with his wisdom and understanding, me included, but I think you are destined to do the same."

CHAPTER TWENTY-FIVE

I have a dream that my four little children will one day live in a nation where they will not be judged by the color of their skin, but by the content of their character.

—Martin Luther King Jr.

Now that I'm back in Atlanta, I divide my time judiciously between continuing to write articles about Samuel, writing editorials concerning equal rights, and now writing editorials concerning the plight of Jews in Europe. I find myself with little time to spend with Allison.

Our relationship has changed appreciably. It has become obvious to us both and many of our business associates that we are much more than friends or partners in the fight for equal rights. We have fallen in love, and it seems to be apparent to all.

What little time I find to spend with Allison is usually when I travel. I continue to interview important leaders of the equal-rights movement, traveling to Mississippi, Alabama, and South Carolina.

Even though Samuel's health has improved, I am still concerned about him. I visit him a couple of times each month, and even though he moves about without his wheelchair, I notice his gait is no longer steady and strong as it was a few months back.

It is the first of December, and Atlanta is in a tizzy about the premiere of *Gone with the Wind*. On December 13, the stars begin to arrive in Atlanta. Ann Rutherford, who played Scarlett O'Hara's sister Carreen O'Hara, is first to arrive in Atlanta. She comes into Terminal Station at 10:00 a.m. and is taken by car to the Georgian Terrace hotel, where almost all the movie's stars will stay.

Three o'clock sees the arrival of several major cast members aboard an Eastern Air Lines flight into Candler Field, the Atlanta airport. Among those are Vivien Leigh, who plays Scarlett O'Hara, escorted by Laurence Olivier. Olivia de Havilland and David Selznick and his wife are also on this flight. The guests are whisked off to their rooms at the Georgian Terrace. Governor Rivers declares a three-day holiday, and politicians are asking that Georgians dress in period clothing.

The next day, Clark Gable and his wife, Carole Lombard, arrive at Candler Field and are paraded through Atlanta in a motorcade. Thousands of fans line the street to catch a glimpse of their two favorite celebrities.

I am with Selznick and the governor to witness the parade, and we are at the Georgian Terrace when Gable and Lombard arrive. Selznick and I welcome both celebrities when they arrive, and Gable smiles broadly when he recognizes me. He introduces me to his wife, and then they are hurried away from flashing cameras and the screams of fans.

The actual premiere is tonight; William McKinney and Allison will accompany me to it. I have been informed that we are to sit with the governor and his family, the mayor of Atlanta, and some of the business elite.

After meeting Gable and Lombard at the Georgian Terrace, I stroll over to Loew's Theatre, where the premiere is to be held. The theatre itself is swarming with activity. I notice hundreds of employees cleaning, straightening, and decorating the opulent theatre. I notice that almost all are colored. I find it odd that their talents and their abilities are welcomed to be a part of preparation but that they will not be allowed to view the results of their hard work at the premiere. I write a note to myself about this.

I see a group of young colored boys escorted off a bus and marched through the stage entrance of the theatre. The boys are in everyday street attire but are carrying what appear to be choir robes. I am curious, so I follow. The young boys, led by a several adult negroes, are allowed in, and I attempt to just follow them through the door as if I am part of the entourage. A policeman stationed at the stage entrance stops me and says, "Excuse me, sir. I must see your pass to allow you to enter."

I flash my press pass to the older officer, and he studies it. He says, "I'm sorry, but the press is not allowed in now. Only those involved with the actual production, for rehearsal's sake, are allowed in."

"I am a guest of the producer, David Selznick. I have just left him at the Georgian Terrace, and he has requested me to report on the preparations. If you are inclined, you are welcome to call the Georgian Terrace and verify my reason for being here."

I was bluffing, and I felt as if I was doing a poor job of it, for even though it was a terribly cold day, I was sweating profusely—not to mention that my bluffing verbiage was more of a stutter.

The officer stepped inside the door and produced a clipboard with several sheets of paper attached. He seemed to review it for a moment and then shook his head no. He questioned, "What was your name again?"

I stammer, "Jonathan Newcastle, from the *New York Times*."

The officer glances at me and then smiles. He says, "You're the one that is writing the story about the negro slave that became a Cherokee—Samuel, I think, was the name?"

"Yes, sir."

"I love reading the story. Please go right in."

Once in, I enter a short hallway, following signs pointing to the stage. I have difficulty maneuvering through the crowd of workers, but I eventually come across the group of young colored boys standing patiently just behind where one would enter the stage itself. One of the adult men of the group appears to be briefing the young boys, and just as I approach to introduce myself, the adult man says, "Let us pray."

Immediately the young boys bow their heads in prayer, and even though I have not been noticed by the group, my proximity to them seems to insist I bow my head as well.

"In Jesus Christ's name, amen!" the adult proclaims, and the young boys chime their amens as well.

I step forward and introduce myself to the adult leader. I say, "Excuse me, sir. I'm Jonathan Newcastle from the *New York Times.* I am curious as to your purpose here. You appear to have quite a following of young, good-looking men. I'm just curious why."

The man, who appears to be close to forty years old, smiles a guarded smile. He offers his hand and says, "I'm Martin Luther King, pastor of Ebenezer Baptist Church. Our purpose—well, our youth boys' choir is here to rehearse, for they are to perform for the premiere tonight."

I am shocked, for I assumed there would be no negroes allowed to be a part of the active premiere. Even though I'm shocked by the revelation, I am elated. I say, "That is magnificent! I can't wait to hear their performance. I will be pleased to report this great news to my good friend Samuel. He will be most pleased."

The pastor stares at me for a moment and says, "Samuel? Samuel who?"

"Oh, I must apologize. I am so excited about your group performing, I lost my head for a moment. I have a friend, Samuel Timmons, who will be most excited about this performance."

Reverend King smiles and says, "I know Samuel Timmons! He is one of my closest friends. Will he be attending tonight?"

"Unfortunately, no, for he has been ill and is unable to travel, but I assure you, I will give him all the details of the premiere and especially the news of you and your group of young men."

The whole time we are speaking, there is a young negro boy clinging to the reverend's side. He is staring at me throughout our conversation. I look at the young boy and say, "You must be very proud to have been chosen to be a part of such an event."

The pastor smiles and says, "I'm sorry. This is my son Martin Luther King Jr. This is his first year in our boys' choir. He is proud, I assure you. Please, you must stay and watch us rehearse. I will be curious to your opinion of the talent of our young choir."

"I would be honored to be a part of the rehearsal. May I ask you something? It's rather controversial though."

The reverend nods yes.

"You and your young men have been chosen to perform for the premiere. To my knowledge, your group will be the only negroes allowed to attend or perform. Even several of the negro actors and actresses of the movie itself are being excluded. Why is it that you're allowed but others are not—at least, in your opinion?"

"We are here to deliver God's message and that alone. To God, our Father, we are all his children. White, black, or whatever, the message is all the same. It should not make any difference who speaks God's word, for the word cannot be denied. That's the best explanation I can give."

The young boys are lined up on the stage, and they rehearse two hymns, which I find most beautiful. The Reverend Martin Luther King appears proud of their efforts, and before they stroll offstage he makes his way back to me. He shakes my hand and says,

"Please tell Samuel that I am praying for him and that I love him dearly."

The premiere is an elegant event. I wear a tuxedo, as does most of the audience. Allison wears a beautiful evening gown, looking gorgeous. I think I even catch Gable himself staring at her.

The young negro boys' choir that had I watched earlier in the day performs their two hymns, which draws tremendous applause from the packed theatre.

I find the movie itself very entertaining, as does Allison. There are several scenes in the movie that elicit cheers of approval. I cannot help but compare how the movie depicts slavery to the way Samuel had described it to me, but I refrain from mentioning it to anyone during the film, nor do I mention it afterward. I feel it best to allow everyone involved to simply bask in the glory, at least for this evening.

Allison, William McKinney, and I attend several parties following the premiere, and I can talk to most of the cast. I try to keep my conversations with the famous stars general and casual. I do not want to appear as if I am taking advantage of being invited to corner them and discuss controversial topics, thus ruining their festivities.

Several of the cast, Gable for one, have read some of the story about Samuel, and almost all have read the editorial about the Jewish refugees. They all applaud my efforts in bringing these horrific events to the public's attention, and even though I do not bring up any of these controversial topics of discussion, they do so with enthusiasm most willingly.

In the next few days, I write an article describing in detail the opulent event. The article merely tells the facts and contains no personal or political opinion of the event. I send the article right away for review and possible printing to the *New York Times.* It appears in the paper the next day.

I write several editorials discussing the political, social, and racial aspects of the premiere, and these I must take great care with, for I do not want to appear as if I'm browbeating others with my opinions. Samuel has taught me to simply provide alternative considerations to such controversial topics. "Plant the seeds, and feel what the new season might bring"—I think this is how he described it.

What little I do know is that the new season will bring war—not only to Europe but to the world—and I will be a part of it.

CHAPTER TWENTY-SIX

To be heroic is to be courageous enough to die for something; to be inspirational is to be crazy enough to live a little.

—Criss Jami

It is mid-January of 1940 when Harold Sims contacts me from New York and says, "I want to run something by you."

I know that since my editorials are doing well, I may be up for some sort of promotion or at least a substantial raise. I fear they will offer me an advancement of some sort that would require me to move back to New York. If a move is required, I know I probably will accept anyway, especially if the pay increase is substantial, although I would miss being near Allison. The more I think about it, the less I think I would move.

Sims approaches our conversation very carefully. He makes small talk, praises me for my achievements, and in a rambling way finally makes known the real reason for the call. He says, "Jonathan, as you know, Germany has begun to invade Poland, and it appears they do not plan to stop there. Great Britain has been building their army, navy, and air corps in response and has already begun sending troops to France in anticipation of a German invasion. Specifically, the British Expeditionary Force has been assembling along the French and Belgium border in response to Germany's aggression. I have been asked to send someone who I think is most qualified to report on these activities. I don't think I have to tell you that this assignment, if you accept it, should be considered hazardous, for you will be embedded with a front-line infantry unit of the British force. It would involve you leaving immediately, at least within the next two weeks, and travel to Somerset, England, to be trained in light infantry with the Tenth Battalion."

With this said, Sims is quiet. He seems to be waiting to hear my initial opinion of the proposal. I am taken by surprise, and I'm at a loss for words. Sims continues, "Jonathan, I know this has come as a surprise to you, but I must tell you that if you want to advance your career substantially, then this is an opportunity you should consider. There are a handful of others I can offer this to, but I truly believe you are the most qualified and have the most passion to write about the horrors of such a conflict. I will be more than happy to give you some time to consider this proposal. I would rather you not make a hasty decision, given its importance and risk."

"Harold, I appreciate your confidence in me. This has come as a surprise. I know that sometime soon, the United States will be involved in the conflict as well, and I had already mentally prepared myself for that. This proposal is a complete surprise, and I need a little time to think about it and to talk it over with...loved ones."

When I finish this statement, I first think of Allison and what she will think, and then Samuel, and only after that do I think of my parents. I think that is odd.

Sims says, "I understand, Jonathan. Please take the time you feel necessary, but understand we must act fairly rapidly."

"Yes, of course, Harold. I will let you know as soon as possible." And we hang up.

I immediately call Allison and tell her the news. She is not the least bit happy about it. I call Samuel, and he is quiet for too long. I know he is going to think I am absurd to even consider it, and he confirms my intuition. My parents surprise me. They seem to be very accepting of the idea; after all, many young men my age will be in battle before long. They seem to think being a war correspondent might be a better alternative than an actual infantryman in the war.

I spend the rest of the day thinking of my options and the concerns of the people I love.

That evening, I take Allison to dinner, and the mood seems to be very somber. I think she knows already that I will accept the assignment, regardless of what she might argue. As always, she is right.

The next day, I travel to Qualla to meet with Samuel. I want to discuss this issue with him personally. There is no one with whom I would rather confer than him over this matter. I am anxious as to what he might say.

Midmorning, I arrive at his small house in Qualla, and we sit by his wood-burning stove and smoke our pipes.

As I describe the proposal to him, he listens intently. He studies me closely as I describe the situation. He is looking for a weakness or an indecisiveness on my part. He eventually says, "The biggest mistake that you can make is to believe that you are working for somebody else. The driving force of a career must come from you. Remember, your job is owned by the company; you own your career! Your concern is to know what your career is to be, and then give yourself to it with all your heart. If you have an undeniable desire to tell the horrors of war for the right reasons, then I understand your willingness to do this, but you should not do it for any other reason. No amount of money or fame is worth the sacrifice."

I leave Samuel late in the afternoon, and this farewell seems different. He hugs me a little tighter, maybe a little longer than usual, and he whispers in my ear, "*Gvgeyu'i.*"

I'm not sure what it means, but on my way, out of Qualla, I stop at a small grocery and question the cashier. From her appearance, I assume her to be Cherokee, so I ask, "Excuse me, ma'am. May I ask you what 'Gvgeyu'i' might mean in Cherokee?" I try to reproduce the pronunciation of Samuel.

The lady smiles and says, "I am impressed with your Cherokee, young man. It means, 'I love you.'"

The three-hour drive from Qualla to Atlanta seems much longer, for I cannot think of anything other than the decision I must make. I think of Allison, and I think of what Samuel has said. Not far out of Qualla, a light snow begins to fall. The large flakes float lazily in front of my headlights as I maneuver through the mountain roads. There is a stillness, a quietness, that seems to herald the decision I am about to make.

Thirty minutes outside of Atlanta, the snow stops. There is only a light dusting on the ground, and I decide to drive directly to Allison's house, for I have made my decision, and I feel a responsibility to explain my decision to her.

I know that if I do not accept the assignment, someone else will, and I am afraid that this person may not report what matters most in a situation of war. I know I am the best for this assignment and would be doing the public—which needs to know the truth—a disservice to refuse. I feel confident in my decision.

I tell Allison of my decision. I tell Allison what Samuel has said and my reasoning for eventually deciding to accept the assignment. She cries.

She cries because she fears for my life. She cries because she will miss me immensely. She cries because our work on equal rights will end. She cries because she loves me.

I call Sims the next morning and inform him I am ready to accept the assignment in England. I can leave whenever the arrangements can be made. I know I sound more confident than I am, for I am scared. I am scared to death of what I am bringing myself to be a part of.

Fewer than two weeks later, I find myself in Somerset, England. Somerset is a small town in the southwestern part of England. It is a quaint town with all the amenities of any moderate-size town in the States. The streets are teeming with activity. There are hundreds of soldiers milling about the town, and I realize that very soon, I will be one of them.

I am taken to the military base where my training will begin.

After my processing, my paperwork, my physical exam, and my written aptitude test (which I think a second grader could have completed with a perfect score), I am assigned to my unit, the Tenth Infantry Brigade.

They don't tell me where we will be sent eventually; they only tell me what they tell the other members of the brigade, and that is where we are to be and what we are to wear the next hour.

I find the training grueling, and it lasts over a period of eight weeks. We are given very little leave, and there is virtually no time for me to write of my experiences. I begin to think I have misjudged this assignment miserably.

I miss Allison tremendously, and I do manage to write small notes here and there and mail them to her, which she will probably receive several weeks later. During the eight weeks of training, I receive ten letters from her. I find them heartwarming, and I reread them so many times that I can recite each letter verbatim. I find this very telling of her true fondness for me, and I realize more than ever my monumental love for her.

After the initial eight weeks of infantry training, I am sent to London where the headquarters for war correspondents is located.

I spend four weeks there mastering their communication procedures and learning the proper chain of command for war correspondents in the field. I wear the British Expeditionary Force's uniform, have officer status, and must answer to the superiors of the armed forces unit of which I am a part. I do not carry a weapon, although I have learned how to use the Browning automatic rifle proficiently during my basic training. I will be a part of the Tenth Brigade in all regards except for carrying a weapon. In accordance with the Geneva Convention, a journalist or war correspondent cannot be willfully targeted by an enemy.

On May 14, 1940, the Tenth Light Infantry Brigade sets sail for France. We land at Dunkirk and immediately board trucks to be convoyed to the French-Belgian border. There is a light armored division that accompanies us, and I am not sure if it is for our safety or if they are also a part of the total defensive line that we are to form along the border.

I find my journalistic urges overwhelmed by the sheer amount and uniqueness of information a combat unit in war provides. There is so much to report that it creates a sense of frustration. It takes me a few days to realize that I must choose my topic of focus and, at least for now, ignore the rest. I decide to interview and talk at length with my fellow soldiers. I ask them about their fears, about their beliefs, about their opinions of Hitler, the Jews, and the war. I describe the soldiers' faces and their demeanors as we move closer and closer to the war zone. I tell of the young soldier who carries a small photograph of his young wife; it is so worn from him constantly viewing and handling it that the image has all but disappeared. His name is Private William Hall. He was just married three months before and has recently received notice that his wife is pregnant. He seems to be the most fearful of the group, and on many occasions, I have heard him crying in the night. He has told me he misses his wife beyond belief, but he now must cope with the possibility of dying in battle, having never seen his child.

My best friend is Connor O'Malley, who comes from Edinburgh, Scotland. He is about my age and is quite the jokester. We became best friends in our initial training at Somerset. I think I find myself drawn to him because of his lighthearted attitude and his amiability. He is a large, muscular man, standing well over six feet, and with his red hair, he gives the appearance of a ferocious barbarian, although I know him to be otherwise.

After several days of travel, the Tenth Brigade comes to form a line of defense, which includes a division of the Belgian army to the left and a division of the French army to the right. Our line of defense stretches from Leuven to Wavre in Belgium, just west of the Dyle River. The area we occupy is rural with gentle, rolling hills and green pastures dotted with an occasional cow; there are a few farm houses in between. It is beautiful country, not much different from what I am accustomed to in the States. I imagine that where we lie in wait would normally be serene, quiet, and peaceful, but now, with the constant groan of machinery from the large number of trucks, artillery, and tanks about the area, there seems to be no escaping reality—the reality that the fire-spitting dragon of war is upon us.

I watch with interest as my comrades ready themselves for battle. I can tell there is an intensified level of anxiety among them, a homogenous mixture of fear and anxiety. There is very little dialogue or discussion of their fears or of what they expect. What they fear the most, I discover, is the lack of will to kill another human being. The Brits have not been brought to the level of anger or hate. They simply move and react; they obey the orders that are spat from a radio in the command post. The radio crackles with static, and the voice, sometimes not discernible, barks commands. All we can do is hold our breath and say a silent prayer.

The French move about with an angered anxiety, for they are defending their doorstep. They know it is only them between the fire-spitting dragon of the German army and their land. They are ready to fight for their lives and their loved ones.

One evening, I question my friend Connor about my observations. I say, "O'Malley, do you hate the Germans? Do you feel anger toward them?"

O'Malley shuffles in his foxhole and glances my way. He shakes his head and says, "No, Newcastle, I don't think I have ever felt hate toward anyone."

"Neither have I, O'Malley, and that makes me wonder if we are prepared for war."

The next morning, O'Malley and I shuffle about in the first few rays of the morning sun. We stroll to one of the lorries, hoping to get a biscuit and maybe some ham but for sure a cup of coffee. The lorry is parked about a hundred yards down the road, and we walk leisurely toward it.

As we top a small knoll of the one lane road, we spot two villagers running toward us. They are screaming and appear to be running for their lives. O'Malley, not knowing their purpose, draws his rifle and commands them to halt. They keep running. The two villagers are pointing behind them and toward the air. At that moment, I hear O'Malley's rifle explode; I see what they are running from. The skies are filled with parachutes falling lazily toward the ground in silence. They are German soldiers.

I can spot the German O'Malley had fired upon, for he is hanging limp in his harness, and he hits the ground with a thud not thirty yards from where we stand.

Immediately, the countryside comes to life. Deafening explosions erupt, rifles blast, and machine guns begin their rhythmic bursts of fire. In a matter of three minutes, our whole line of defense is in disarray. German soldiers seem to sprout from the very ground before us as we jump from one foxhole to the next to find cover.

Between the explosions, smoke, and flying shrapnel, I hear the roar of tanks. They are our tanks, for I recognize the rumble of the engines. O'Malley is firing at will, and I witness him dropping several Germans within a few minutes. I do not know if they are dead, but I assume they are, for they do not attempt to escape the barrage of fire that continues.

Our line of defense begins to develop some order, and our commanders are shouting their orders for us to stand fast! Hold our ground! Let the tanks take on the brunt of the force straightway! We obey but are almost overwhelmed by the German paratroopers who fall from the skies nonstop.

I see our wounded lying all about me, and I do my best to drag them to an empty foxhole or a small depression that will give them some cover. The screams of pain and agony only add to the cacophony that seems to swallow us whole.

I hear the booms of the tanks to our east and see the smoke of the debris that is their target. In the distance, maybe half a mile away, I see a line of tanks come into view along a rolling hill of pasture. There are maybe twenty tanks, and they are German. Hundreds of infantrymen follow the tanks toward us.

Immediately, we are commanded to grab our wounded and retreat at once. We are to retreat to our rear line, which we know to be about a mile behind us to the west.

As I begin to retreat, I spot Private William Hall lying limply in the mud beside the road. I think he is dead, but when I approach, I hear his cries for help. There are still bullets flying about without pause. I hear them whiz by me and hit the ground all around me. How one of the projectiles does not find me is unbelievable. I examine Private Hall quickly and realize he has a severe wound to his left leg. He is bleeding profusely. I tie a tourniquet above the wound and drag him toward our line of retreat. Bullets pepper the ground around us. It seems as if I am caught in a torrential rainstorm of lead as we move slowly through the mud. I try, but I cannot move any faster. It is beyond reason that out of the thousands of bullets that saturate my space, one has not found its target. I glance back to the place where I had found Private Hall a mere three meters away, and I realize that the small photograph of his wife that he so treasures is lying in the mud where he had been. I start to scamper back and retrieve it, but I hear a voice. The voice very calmly and slowly says, "Save him, save yourself, for you both are loved." I recognize the kind, wise voice of Samuel.

I grab Private Hall by his hips and swing him over my shoulder, and with every bit of energy and power I can summon, I run as fast and far as I can to the west.

Our battalion moves westward in retreat along with what is left of the French and Belgian divisions. We stay on the move, allowing us very little sleep or rest. German artillery and dive bombers finds us so frequently that we wear our tin hats continuously, even when we sleep. Each time we seek cover from the barrage of fire the Germans send our way, we emerge from the rubble and smoke and realize that there are considerably less of us to retreat. I find it terribly sad.

⟡

One evening, my good friend Connor and I are talking, resting among the rubble of an old farmhouse. The barrage of artillery and bombing has seemed to cease temporarily. I question him, "O'Malley, do you hate the Germans now?"

Once again, he shakes his head almost in disgust and says, "No. Now I hate myself."

It will take us eight days to make our way to Dunkirk on the coast of France. A plan has been developed to evacuate the British soldiers who had been part of the battle of France from Dunkirk, and eventually there will be over three hundred thousand soldiers rescued from the advancing Germans. Of the 150,000 British Expeditionary Force, 68,000 are either dead, wounded, missing, or captured. O'Malley and I carry the stretcher of Private William Hall aboard the *HMS Calcutta* on June 4.

That night, I stand on the deck of the *Calcutta* and stare at the star-filled sky. Other than the sound of the wind, the waves breaking against the hull, and an occasional clink of metal, there is silence. It is as if the war had been erased or at the very least has come to an end. At that moment, I think of Samuel, and once again I hear him say, "Save him, save yourself, for both of you are loved." I smile and take a long draw from my pipe, and then out of the stillness and silence, I hear the stars sing their melody.

CHAPTER TWENTY-SEVEN

The fear of death follows from the fear of life. A man who lives fully is prepared to die at any time

—Mark Twain

We are back in Dover, England, the following day. It's a rainy day; the wind whips about as we disembark the ship. We look as if we are a defeated lot, which I guess we are. There are several ships of all sizes unloading other troops like ourselves. The tanks, lorries, and other equipment are noticeably absent, for during our fast retreat, they were left in the fields and alongside the roads of Belgium and France.

We are taken by convoy to a base just west of Dover near the small town of Shepherdswell and are given care. We are fed, assigned to barracks, and told to rest till we get further orders.

We all expect we will be deployed again soon. Even though we try to rest and prepare ourselves mentally to be redeployed, we all find it difficult, for now we know the reality of war.

A month goes by, and most of my comrades spend the days playing soccer, traveling into town for a beer, or, for those that live not too far away, traveling home to be with family. I spend my time writing. I write Allison a letter every day telling her of my experiences, although I downplay the reality of the violence, for I do not want to worry her unnecessarily. I write Samuel a couple of letters a week describing my comrades, the war, and my own emotions concerning them. I hope he reads them and sends me his advice.

I write article after article for the *New York Times* about my observations of the Battle of France. British journalists have written that the evacuation of the British Expeditionary Forces from Dunkirk was a triumph. Churchill himself claimed it as a tremendous victory. The evacuation became known as Operation Dynamo. I wondered how anyone can claim victory when, of the 150,000 British troops, over 3,500 were killed; 13,000 were wounded; and one out of seven soldiers was captured. I think they consider it a victory because at least some soldiers, myself included, lived to tell about it.

I receive letters almost every day. I get one from Allison almost daily. These I read over and over. I find she has a way with her writing that projects her tenderness with such clarity that I cannot help but get emotional. I have gotten a few from Samuel, and his letters tend to be very general. He tells me of his garden, his neighbors, and his friends and will usually ask at least one pointed question about the war or my experiences. I think he is reluctant to know the entire description of the horror. Also in his letters, he will always sneak in a thought to ponder, a thought that I will usually find helpful in dealing with my emotions concerning this war.

In September, I receive a wire from Allison that informs me that Samuel has been readmitted into the hospital. It is not very detailed; it reads simply, "Samuel back in hospital. Very dire."

I go to the commander and request a temporary leave to travel back to the States, which he approves.

It takes me a week to eventually get back to Atlanta. I am so excited to be back home, even if it is for just a little while. I am worried about Samuel, and I have an urge to immediately go to the hospital to be by his side, but I also feel a desperate need to be with Allison. I need to feel her hug, her touch, and her tender kiss, for I have seen too many atrocities. I need to feel some normalcy. I want to forget what I have seen.

Allison hugs me so tightly that it takes my breath away. She buries her head against my chest and cries silently. I kiss her tenderly, a kiss as soft as a dewdrop on a rose petal. Nothing is spoken, for there are no words that can capture what we both feel.

Allison breaks the silence and whispers, "Please never leave me again. I love you too much to lose you." It is only a whisper, an audible thought, but she's pleading.

"I love you too." I want to tell her I will never leave, but I know better. I know I am to return. This is merely a temporary reprieve from the nightmare of war.

We go to see Samuel at the hospital. He is in coronary intensive care. Apparently, he has had a heart attack, and the prognosis is not too promising. He is very weak, and at first, the nurses do not want to let me in to see him, but after I plead my case, they allow me to enter.

If it had not been for Samuel's unique look, the long white hair and white beard, I would not have known it was him. He has withered to half his normal size and is sleeping in a fetal position. I touch his hand softly. He opens one eye and then the other. He smiles a meek smile. I say, "Hello Samuel, how about a walk? Maybe a walk to the top of Wayah?"

He laughs breathlessly, coughs, and attempts to right himself in the bed. His eyes have lost their shine, the glimmer that I had been so fond of. He says very weakly, "I hope you brought proper shoes this time, Jonathan."

I laugh and hold his hand in mine. We simply stare at one another, for he is too weak to speak, and I am too weary of trying to find the right words that comfort those near death. I have seen too much death, too much sorrow, and now I am spent of the words to comfort the person I have grown to love the most.

Samuel says, "We must talk, Jonathan. There is much I need to tell you. The war…" And then he falls asleep.

The nurse is standing by my side. She nods at me and says, "Please, Mr. Newcastle, he is very weak. Maybe come back tomorrow morning. He is usually a little more chipper then."

"Yes. Of course. I'll be back tomorrow."

As I drive back to Allison's house, I think about the short conversation I just had with Samuel. The last few words he spoke were "We must talk. There is much I need to tell you." Then he said, "The war." I know he wants to tell me something about the war, something important, for I could tell in the tone of his voice.

I have dinner with Allison and her grandfather William at one of our favorite restaurants. Having been deprived of good American food, I eat ravenously, almost as if I have not eaten at all for months. Allison and William both seem to find it humorous.

William questions me about the war, and I give him snippets of the occurrences. I want to tell him the details, the absolute atrocities I had seen, but I want to spare Allison the details. I give a very sterilized account of the events and attempt to change the subject instead.

I catch Allison studying me on occasion. I think she knows I am paling the description of the events, and it makes me feel a little uncomfortable, for I do not wish her to think I am a liar. I take my pipe out and take a long puff and say, "I find nothing about war that warrants a discussion, other than the one to discredit its reason."

Allison grabs my arm and squeezes it tightly with her hand. William smiles and nods. He says, "Spoken as a true gentleman."

The next morning, I arrive at the hospital before normal visiting hours. The nurses check on Samuel to make sure he is awake and lucid and then allow me in to see him.

He seems much more aware this morning. He smiles and says, "Did you bring your pipe, Jonathan?"

"Yes, Samuel."

"Then, please, let's have a smoke."

I fill the bowl of my pipe and light it. I take a long drag and hand the pipe to Samuel. He takes a long draw of the pipe, and the bowl glows red. His eyes begin to gleam as well. He says, "I need to talk with you about the war…and Allison."

I pull up a chair and nod.

Samuel says, "There will come a time where you must make choices. You will be torn between fulfilling Allison's dreams and fulfilling your own. These choices can be most difficult, for I know how much you love Allison. I can see it in your eyes. I will tell you that you must choose to follow your passion, your dreams, your purpose in life, for those are the very things she loves about you. It can be most difficult to understand. I will tell you, that I too do not ever want you to leave, but I know your dreams, your purpose in life, and I admire and love that about you. Do you understand, Jonathan?"

I pull my chair a little closer and say, "I know where I should be, but I want to be with her. I want to always be with her, to hold her, to have children, and to grow old. If I do what I should and follow my passion, I may never return. I am only here now because I was lucky. There were many times I should have been killed, as many of my friends were in battle. What would my death accomplish?"

"No one ever has a choice about death. It will happen to us all. Our choice is only how to live. If you live your life to fulfill your dreams, then death is only a reprieve from those ideals."

I nod; I am beginning to understand. I know this in my own mind, but it sounds much more logical coming from Samuel. I say, "And what would Gawonii say?"

Samuel smiles and says, "He told Peter and me this: 'You hear the stars sing. Now you must listen to what they are saying, for there is where you will find the answer.'"

I tell Samuel I will see him tomorrow, and I go to meet Allison. She has planned an outing for us both, a picnic along the Chattahoochee River in a park. It will be a nice relief from the difficult emotions of Samuel's demise and of the hard decisions that I must make.

It is a fall afternoon, and the leaves are blazing in color. It is a weekday, so the park is almost empty. There are only a few elderly people strolling about. The river flows lazily beside the spot where we decide to sit on our blanket. Allison looks stunning, and I want to hold her close and never let go. I say, "I'm glad I got to come back. There is so much I wanted to say, but felt I could not write my true emotions, of how I felt."

Allison laughs and says, "You're a journalist! A damn good writer! And you could not find the words to write?"

I laugh and sigh. I fidget a bit and say, "Allison, I love you more than you can ever imagine. There has never been anyone that has meant as much to me as you. I want to spend the rest of my life with you...but...I hope you understand that I must go back. I must finish what I started. I must write my story of the war."

Allison begins to cry. She tries to hide her tears, but I know. I say, "I'm sorry, Allison. I do love you, but—"

Allison says, "Please, Jonathan, stop! It is so stupid! If you go, I will probably never...never see you again! And I'm supposed to accept that?"

"I will come back, I promise."

"And your friends that you were with in Belgium. Did they say the same to their loved ones, their wives? The friends that were left on the battlefield? I'm not stupid, Jonathan. I know what happened. Am I to smile and simply wish you well? What about me?"

"Whether I die today or tomorrow or live to be one hundred years old like Samuel, I want you to be proud of what I am. I can never be the one to decide when I die, but I can decide how I should live. I want to live to be the person you apparently love. I will return."

Allison cries and buries her head in my arms. I hold her close and wonder if I am making the right choice, and for some reason I think of Ahyoka and Samuel.

Over the next two weeks, I see Samuel almost every day in the mornings, and the rest of my time is spent with Allison. The topics of my going back to England and the war seem to be what we talk mostly about, and Allison never seems to agree. I question Samuel about this matter, and he simply shrugs his shoulders and says, "I have had only one love in my life. I am not much of a ladies' man, Jonathan. I have had very little experience in matters such as this." And he smiles.

A few days before I am to return to England, Allison asks, "Do you love me, Jonathan?"

"Yes, of course. More than you will ever know."

"You say you love me, but you will return to the war regardless of what I say, will you not?"

"What you say will always weigh heavily on me, but yes, I must return to what I know is my calling."

She begins to cry and whimpers, "Then, please, marry me before you go. Please, at least give me that."

I hold her close and say, "Yes, I will marry you, and I will come back. I promise." After I say this, I think of Private William Hall. I think of the small photograph that he carried with him and the fear he had of never returning to his love. I now feel the same fear.

A week later, I marry Allison. There is not much of a ceremony. We simply go to the courthouse and invite a few of our friends to be present, and it is done. Even though Samuel's condition has been stabilized, he is not able to attend the wedding, and this troubles me greatly. I am happy that my parents could travel from New York to be with us, and I, as well as Allison, notice that they seem to treat me differently than before. It seems like they, for once, are proud of what I have become. I'm not sure if it is because I am getting married or if it is the fact that they see a different man in me since my experiences in the war.

Our honeymoon is short, only three days, for I have to return to England. We stay two nights at the Georgian Terrace in one of their most luxurious suites. The bellboy who handles our few bags tells us that it is the same room in which Clark Gable and his wife, Carole Lombard, had stayed during the premiere of *Gone with the Wind.*

The morning I am to fly out of Atlanta is very sad. Allison cries uncontrollably, and it troubles me beyond belief to leave her weeping in her grandfather's arms. I stop by the hospital to see Samuel. He smiles and says, "Please, Jonathan, let us smoke."

I light my pipe, and we pass it back and forth without many words said, for we both know that this will most likely be the last time we share the pipe.

Samuel says, "I am proud of you, Jonathan. You are a much better didanawisgi than I. Do you remember what tohi means?"

"Yes, Samuel. It means wellness and peace."

"The Great Spirit will favor you, for you will bring the spirit of tohi to others. Your choice to pursue this purpose in life is admirable, but it can be overwhelming. You must strive to bring tohi to one man, one child, just one soul at a time. To try to bring it to the masses is like trying to count the stars at night. Do you understand, my son?"

"Yes, Samuel. I do."

Samuel smiles and reaches to hug me. I kneel to his bedside and embrace his frail frame. I whisper in his ear, "Gvgeyu'i." *I love you.*

EPILOGUE

I return to England and my unit, the Tenth Infantry Brigade. London is continuously bombarded by the Germans, and it creates havoc among the civilian population. In 1941, we are deployed to North Africa and become involved in the Tunisia Campaign. Most of the battles we are involved with during the Tunisia campaign are very costly as far as human life. The battles are short but intense and take many lives on both sides, but in the end, the Allies claim victory.

One of the deciding factors in the Tunisia Campaign is logistics. The ability to transport supplies, fuel, food, and ammunition is hampered by the sheer lack of adequate ports along the North African coast. Unfortunately, mail is also hampered by the same logistical issues, and I at times will go a month before receiving one piece of mail. I miss reading Allison's lovely thoughts.

Two months after arriving in North Africa, I receive several letters from Allison. The first I read is postmarked from the previous month and tells me that Samuel has passed away. I am very distraught by the news and by the fact that I receive the news in such an untimely fashion. I begin to question my reason for being here.

I read the next letter. Allison informs me that she is pregnant. I am to be a father.

In 1943, the Tenth Infantry, having claimed victory in North Africa, deploys to the Italian Campaign. The United States has joined forces with the Allies and has begun to send troops to North Africa and now to the Italian Campaign as well. I request a transfer from my British unit to the Eighty-Second Armored Reconnaissance Battalion of the US Army.

The Eighty-Second Armored Reconnaissance is the same battalion that my friend Private Stafford is a part of. I am surprised that we crossed paths with our taking of Palermo, Italy. It is nice to have someone from the past to talk with. The three friends who had been with him on the train from Asheville unfortunately had been killed in North Africa.

In June of 1944, the Eighty-Second is redeployed and becomes part of the Normandy landings on Omaha Beach.

North Africa, Italy, and now Normandy have taken their tolls on American and British lives. I have seen so much death that one would think that I have grown accustomed to it, but one never gets use to such devastation and sorrow.

I lose contact with my friend Connor O'Malley after I leave the Tenth Infantry of the British Expeditionary Force. I hope he has survived, for he is a good man and a good soldier. I credit him with saving my life on many occasions.

Private Hall, the wounded soldier I carried from the battlefield in Belgium, survives his wounds and is medically discharged and sent home. I get a letter from him in the last few days of the war and am proud to know that he is now the father of three young boys.

I come home much earlier than many of my comrades in the Eighty-Second. They stay in Europe and operate as part of an occupational force till mid-1946.

I come home to Allison and our son in June of 1945. Our son is four years old when I first meet him. I think he looks like me, but it seems he has Allison's disposition. We name him Samuel.

A year after my return, Allison and I are awarded a second son, whom I insisted we name Peter, and two years later, we have a daughter, whom Allison insisted she name. Allison names her Abigail; we call her Abbey.

I receive many awards for my writings of the war. I receive the Pulitzer for journalism in 1946 and take a new position as chief editor for *Look* magazine, which does not require as much travel.

Much of my effort, even with the new position of chief editor, is still directed at promoting equal rights for all. I take great pride in the small, almost insignificant changes I have influenced in the public's opinions. I think often of Samuel and his advice and understand now, more than ever, what he meant when he told me to realize that one man, one child, or one soul enlightened is worth the effort. I still hear him often sharing his wisdom. I hear him within the stars.

Both Allison and I spend much of our free time with the children and have found much happiness in this alone. I love to read to them. They beg me every night to read them a story or sometimes to simply tell them a story. I have read all the classic stories that children adore: *The Adventures of Pinocchio, Cinderella, Alice in Wonderland,* and many others. Most nights, the three of them will plead for me to tell them their favorite story. They enjoy the adventure, the magic, and the sweetness of the strange fairy tale that is my favorite as well. It is a story I tell with much emotion, for it is about an old, wise man named Samuel.

86190566R00126

Made in the USA
Columbia, SC
08 January 2018